THE SWEET ROAD
TO LOVE

<u>**THE SWEET ROAD TO LOVE**</u>

Other Books By Jacki Kelly

THE SWEET ROAD SERIES
The Sweet Road Home
The Sweet Road Back

DATING JUST GOT SERIOUS
Blind Date
One Date At A Time
Date Me
A Single Date
Speed Date
Dating Just Got Serious – Box Set
Done With Dating

WOMEN'S FICTION
Packed and Ready To Go
Going Backwards

Chapter One

Her life had turned into a rerun that nobody wanted to see. She winced as scenes scrolled through her head. Dakota Conroy looked around her drab bookstore and sighed. The only hint of color was on the back wall, but the orange paint was faded and peeling. Out of all the stores on Main Street in Bristol, Delaware, hers had the same run-down look as her life. The frayed upholstered chairs and nicked wooden bookshelves looked as bad as she felt. What she needed was a spark of something fresh.

Her last customer circled the end cap of books and made her way back down the romance aisle. If she didn't make a selection soon, Dakota vowed to do it for her.

"Uh, Ms. Donald, we closed twenty minutes ago. If you can't find something you like, I can make a selection for you. We put together our weekly reading list this morning," Dakota called as the woman opened another book and stared at the pages.

"Oh, sweetie, I'll know it when I find it. Don't you fret about me. Just go on and do what you need to do." She gave Dakota a dismissive wave

Dakota cut her eyes away. "Yeah, but would you be happy if I locked you in here tonight?" she mumbled as she closed the register.

"What was that?"

"Oh, nothing. Tell you what…consider those books in your hand a gift from me."

"What's your hurry tonight?" Ms. Donald dropped the books on the counter and watched as Dakota bagged her purchase.

"I'm expecting a call." Dakota wished she was more excited about hearing from Brian, but their conversations were just a rehash and she hung up always wanting more.

Dakota walked out of the bookstore behind Ms. Donald and locked the door. If she didn't hurry, she would miss the call. Another whole week of waiting before she heard from him again was about as appealing as traffic court.

She parallel parked in front of her house and ran up the stairs. Inside, she ditched her coat and purse in the hall closet and made her way to the kitchen. Garlic hummus from the refrigerator along with whole grain chips from the pantry made up dinner. At the kitchen counter she used a chip to dig a hunk of the thick spread from the plastic container while staring at the phone.

This was no way to spend another Friday night. Running home from the bookstore, eating dinner from store-bought containers. In the beginning, the waiting was easy. Boasting that her boyfriend was doing volunteer work in Haiti sounded noble, but the varnish on that tale wore thin fast when her friends went on real dates, with real men, to real dinners while she stuck close to home waiting for the phone to ring. She flopped on the sofa and placed her dinner on the coffee table.

With the remote pointed at the television, she turned to her favorite network, HGTV. Halfway through the renovation show, the phone rang.

She answered. "Brian?"

"Hey, Dakota, I can barely hear you."

"How's it going? She spoke louder, relieved to hear his deep baritone voice. She turned off the television to give him her full attention.

"It's good. But conditions here don't seem to change, no matter what we do. There is so much more that needs to be done." His lament was the same lament every week.

"At least you're trying." She tried to keep him encouraged by being the dedicated girlfriend with the pep talk he needed. What she wanted to know was when he planned to come home, but asking seemed selfish when others needed so much help.

"Dakota, I have something to tell you." His voice softened.

"Okay, I'm listening." Dakota hoped she sounded upbeat. If he needed money again to help out another family, she wanted him to feel okay asking her for the donation.

Static crackled across the line.

"It's…long…I'm…coming…I…to…Central …"

"Brian, you're breaking up again." She spoke louder, hoping he could hear her. "Can you call me back?" She sat on the edge of the sofa, knowing the call would get disconnected soon.

"I…remote."

"Brian, I can't hear you." She held the receiver away from her ear and looked at device. "Brian?" She shook the phone. "Brian?"

The line went dead. She continued to hold the phone, hoping for something magical to happen.

What was he trying to say? There was something different about his tone. Maybe after a year of volunteerism, he was ready to come home and start a real life with her.

What did he expect her to do? Be miserable too, in order to show her dedication to him? What was the acceptable time limit before she could complain about being alone?

After several minutes, she put the phone down and made her way to the refrigerator. She peered inside for something else to eat. Filling the empty pit in her stomach might ease the loneliness a little. Dakota grabbed an apple and bit it while leaning against the counter. He'd sounded so serious. There was something in his tone that demanded attention.

Chapter Two

A whole week and not a word from Brian. Even for him that was unusual. Dakota parked the car in front of the store and surveyed the exterior. The windows needed cleaning. Dust clung to the large plate glass like a film. How could customers see all the wonderful books inside? Today, she'd have to call the window washers to get them gleaming or do the work herself.

Dakota unlocked the heavy wooden door and stepped inside, then locked it behind her. The store wouldn't open for another hour. Even though the October sun was bright, she flicked the light switch to illuminate the space.

Instead of checking for messages from Brian, she made her way to the small coffee station in the corner. Maybe everything else in the store was antiquated, but the splurge on the latest in brewers had been an excellent purchase. Dakota dropped a decaf hazelnut k-cup into the pocket and pressed the buttons.

When the coffee maker finished brewing, she sweetened the coffee and plopped behind her desk. While the old computer booted up, she sipped from her cup.

Her private line rang, piercing her few moments of serenity before opening the store.

"Dakota, this is Simeon. How are you?" Her brother-in-law's voice sounded businesslike and serious. He seldom called, so he must need something for Asa or Mia.

"I'm surprised you called. What can I do for you?"

"Do you have some free time this afternoon? I have something I want to talk with you about."

"Sure. Do you want to stop by the shop?" She glanced around, noting the pile of books she needed to stack before inviting someone into her tiny office.

"I was hoping you could come here to Harper Enterprise. How about this afternoon at three?

She turned her back on the waiting chores. "Simeon, is everything okay? Is something wrong with Asa or the baby?"

"Dakota, they're fine. I hope I'm not alarming you," he replied.

"Should I come now? I can. Is this about Brian? Is he okay? Did something happen to your brother?" Her voice rose with every question.

"No, nothing happened to Brian. Calm down."

"Can't you just tell me what this is about? I'll be a jumble of nerves all day trying to guess."

"This afternoon would be better. I have some meetings this morning and I've got to drive out to a site. See you at three?"

"Okay. Yes, of course. I'll be there." She stared at the receiver.

§§§

Dakota stepped on the elevator to Simeon's building and punched the button for the twelfth floor. As the elevator doors closed, a hand slipped into the opening, pushing them apart. A tall man with skin the color of pine straw on the forest floor surveyed the space before getting on. He glanced her way, offering her a quick hello, then pressed the already lit twelfth floor button.

Dakota recognized him from a few Harper Enterprise affairs that Asa had invited her to. The only thing missing from him now was the tall, thin beauty usually hanging on his arm. He brought a different one to each occasion. Today, he wore the standard custom-cut business suit with a white starched shirt, looking like a candidate straight from central casting for the role of Leading Man.

8

She glanced down at her rainbow colored rubber boots and faded black jeans. The outfit looked out of place next to him, but going home to change before her meeting with Simeon wasn't an option. She backed into the corner, hoping to go unnoticed by him like she had before.

"So, are you new here?" He turned to face her. His eyes locked on the smidge of midriff showing under her T-shirt. She tugged her top down and pulled her jacket closed. His hand clutched a well-worn leather briefcase. Dakota couldn't help but wonder if his big hands were an indication of other large things. His gorgeous brown skin looked as smooth as fine porcelain and the sexy sound of his voice made her stare at him, hoping he'd say more.

"No, I'm not an employee. I'm meeting with Simeon." She pushed off the wall and tried to stand taller. "I've actually seen you around before."

"Is that right? Where?" The timbre of his voice was made for late-night radio. If she closed her eyes and pretended to be home he could talk her out of her panties.

She continued to look at his mouth. "At the company Christmas party last year and then again at the Independence Day celebration at Asa and Simeon's. Oh, and at the Community Center meeting. But you were very busy with the tall blonde glued to your side."

"Ah, Bridget." His eyes twinkled. "I don't remember seeing you there."

"Yeah, well." She looked down at her comfy jeans. "Let's say you were preoccupied."

The elevator came to a smooth stop and she hopped off. Securing her knapsack on her back, she headed to the large glass doors at the end of the hall. She'd only been to Simeon's office a couple of times with Asa. In the reception area, she half expected to see her sister, but something in Simeon's voice let her know this wasn't a casual visit. This summons didn't have anything to do with Asa. Mr. Handsome from the elevator came up behind her.

"Let me get that door for you." He grabbed the handle before she could reach it.

In place of a thank you, she gave him a nod.

Dakota faced the familiar-looking woman seated behind the receptionist desk. "Hi, I'm Dakota Conroy. I have a meeting with Simeon at three."

"I remember you. You're Simeon's sister-in-law. I'm Catherine. He should be back in a few minutes. Can I get you something to drink while you're waiting?"

"No, I have my own. Thanks." She pulled her reusable water jug from her bag. The deep breathing exercises she'd employed after Simeon's call weren't working to calm her down. Neither were the repeated stares from Mr. Good-looking.

When she took the seat on the sofa, he stepped up to the receptionist desk. From where Dakota sat, she couldn't hear their conversation. She wanted to know his name.

He glanced her way and caught her gawking. Pretending to look at the array of architecture magazines on the table, she picked up one.

After talking with Catherine, he sat across from Dakota and placed his thick leather briefcase between his legs. His shoes gleamed like glass. If his goal was to impress someone, it worked.

Dakota flipped through the pages while stealing glances at him. His sideburns, mustache, and beard grew together in a handsome shade of black that framed his lower face. Mr. Debonair had a smile worth writing about.

"No matter how busy I am, I don't usually miss a pretty face." He flashed a megawatt smile.

"I beg your pardon." Dakota lowered the magazine to peer at him.

"I can't believe I don't remember a woman as beautiful as you."

He had a bag full of compliments at the ready. It must be a requirement for being a playboy. If he got tongue-tied, he couldn't sweep as many women into his fantasy world.

"Oh." She nodded while trying to think of something witty or charming to say. Her mind went blank. That was why she didn't have a pass to that elusive club of players.

"I like those boots. Very colorful." She crossed her legs and wiggled her foot. "They're my favorite. How can I have a bad day when I'm wearing my snazzy footwear?"

"Were you expecting a bad day?"

"It's been a trying week."

"They should make those boots for men. We have bad days too."

"Oh, they make them for men and children." She giggled. "They aren't quite this bright, though. But I must admit I've never seen a man wear a pair. And you certainly don't look like the type."

He faked a chuckle. "What type do I look like?"

She studied him from head to toe. "You're business suits and Italian loafers." She pointed to his shoes, mocking surprise. "See, I'm right. And you probably spit shined them this morning."

"Maybe when I'm having a day off, I could get away with a pair."

She shook her head. "I don't think so."

He stuck out his hand. "I'm Bishop Contee."

"Dakota Conroy. Bishop, that's an unusual name."

"It's a family name. I'm actually Bishop Jamison Contee VII, but since some of those ancestors have passed away, my family doesn't keep such strict count anymore."

"How do you like working for Simeon?"

"I like the diversity of projects and, of course, the people are great. Overall, I'd say this is one of my best contracts. I haven't been with the company too long—just over a year—but if I'd known there were such pretty women like you hanging around the executive offices, I would have started years ago." He managed that compliment with a straight face, almost making her believe him.

"I hardly think you have trouble finding pretty women. You pull them out of your pockets, don't you?" She nestled her chin in the palm of her hand and grinned. Brian couldn't be angry as long as she kept her hands to herself. Besides, Brian hadn't complimented her in months. Maybe never. He was too serious to see the funny side of life.

"A woman with a sense of humor. I like that."

"And you're quite the charmer."

He leaned closer. "Now, why would you say that?"

"Because we've only been sitting here a few minutes and I'm blushing."

"You've got a pretty smile. It would put the Mona Lisa to shame." He moved to the edge of the couch.

"And you've got enough compliments to rival a gigolo."

His burst of laughter sounded so good, she couldn't help but join him.

Simeon pushed through the door. "Hey guys, I'm sorry to keep you waiting, but there were a few problems at the site."

Bishop stood and, side-stepped his briefcase to shake Simeon's hand.

"Dakota, let me speak with Bishop a few minutes, then we can talk. I promise we won't be long."

"No problem. It was nice meeting you, Bishop." She hoped she didn't sound as giddy as she felt.

"It was nicer meeting you." He gave her a warm smile and held her gaze a few seconds before following Simeon into the office.

A quick glance confirmed that his slacks were too loose to give a good view of his butt. She uncrossed her legs. Visions of Bishop would dance in her head tonight. Her stomach tightened with guilt as she tried to conjure up an image of Brian.

Dakota tucked her head down and tried to concentrate on the magazine she held in her lap. Not one of the articles interested her. Fleeting thoughts about a man she just met were ridiculous. She wasn't some horny teenager passing through puberty. She was a thirty-year-old woman in a committed relationship. Even if she wasn't acting like one right now.

The last few conversations with Brian had very little to do with them or their relationship and more to do with money and housing shortages. The photo they'd taken of him at the airport before he went through security seemed hardly recognizable now. She couldn't remember what his lips felt like on hers, or his touch. But even her impetuous side couldn't push her to cheat on Brian. Until he came home, she was stuck.

Walking on stilts had to be easier than trying to maneuver her life right now—unable to reach Brian, Simeon demanding her presence, and a total stranger pushing her to lustful thoughts— all had to be connected, but she couldn't figure out how.

Chapter Three

Bishop settled into the chair in front of Simeon's desk. Hopefully this meeting wouldn't take too long. He wanted to get back to the striking beauty in the reception area.

"How are you settling in?" Simeon asked.

"Good. I'm getting organized. Thanks for offering the office space. Now, when I have several meetings here, I won't have to squat in a conference room. I'm already talking to your staff about other projects." Bishop held his hands together to contain his excitement.

"Catherine has the key for you. Also, I'm scheduling a meeting for next week to discuss the finishing touches on the Community Center. And my wife's is doing a fashion show in New York in a few weeks. I'd like you to check out the set and make sure everything is safe and well built. I don't want any accidents."

Bishop jotted notes. "No problem."

"I don't have much time this afternoon. I really need to talk with my sister-in-law. I don't want to keep her waiting." He glanced at his watch.

"Your sister-in-law?"

"Dakota, yes." Simeon stood up and hesitated for a moment. "This is going to be really tight. I may have to do some juggling."

"Is something wrong?"

"I'll need to give her a ride home after we talk, but I have a meeting with legal in less than an hour. I don't know how I'm going to—"

Bishop stood up. "Let me help. I can take her home for you."

Simeon looked at his watch again and winced. "I don't know. Would you mind doing that for me?"

"No problem. I don't have any appointments until later this afternoon."

Simeon jotted her address on a slip of paper and handed it to him before escorting him to the door. "Thanks. I really appreciate the help. If you can wait for her, we shouldn't be too long."

As they walked out, Dakota sprang out of her seat, so startled that the magazine in her lap fell at her feet.

Bishop walked over, picked it up, and handed the glossy to her along with his brightest smile.

"Thank you." Her voice was lyrical.

He nodded and watched her follow Simeon into the office. She wasn't long and slender like most of the girls he dated, but her butt was nice, round, and the perfect size. She looked like she was smoldering just beneath the surface. All she needed was someone to ignite her blaze. She would probably make good company.

"Bishop, here's the key to your office. It's located down the hall, the first door on the left after the big conference room." Catherine dangled the key on a Harper Enterprise keychain in front of him.

"Thanks. Simeon asked me if I would hang around and give his sister-in-law a ride home."

"Well that's no way to spend your day. Running errands for your boss."

"No, it's not like that. He was going to, but I offered so he could make his meeting this afternoon. I don't mind. She's very pretty."

Catherine lifted one eyebrow, studying his face. "I see. Well, I guess you know what you're doing. But you should know she's dating Simeon's brother." She turned back to her computer and began tapping on the keys.

"Oh...I-I..." He turned around to glimpse the closed door to Simeon's office. He took the seat he'd occupied earlier and intertwined his hands. One less beauty on the market. Too bad. How he'd never noticed those striking features before was odd. Even now, he couldn't wait for her to come back.

He pinched the bridge of his nose. Hard. At least he hadn't said anything to Dakota that could've been considered inappropriate, and he planned to make sure he didn't. The job with Harper Enterprise was too lucrative to screw up. He pulled his cell phone from his pocket and scanned his contact list. He'd find someone else to keep him warm as the weather grew colder. The sudden vibration of his cell phone jolted him back to the present. Sharon's name was displayed on the screen. He shoved the phone back in his pocket. Not now. Not her. Not ever.

§§§

The moment Brian had left, Dakota become invisible. Nobody ever noticed she was in the room. But Bishop Contee had looked at her like she mattered. For the first time in months, she felt her heart racing and the accompanying guilt for wanting more washed over her.

She blinked and focused on her brother-in-law. "I can't wait to find out what was so important that I had to trek down here during the busiest part of my day.”

“I hope I didn’t inconvenient you too much, but I wanted to talk to you in a private place where we wouldn’t be interrupted.” Instead of taking the seat behind his desk in the large leather chair, he sat beside her in the straight back chair facing his desk.

“What is it, Simeon? You’re starting to worry me.”

“How have you been?” He placed his hand on her arm. This was bad news.

She pulled her arm away, crossing them over her chest and glared at him. “Just tell me. Has something happened to Brian?” She unfolded her arms and gripped the sides of the chair. Her head suddenly felt light and unanchored.

“Brian is fine. He sent something for you to listen to.”

“What is it? Why did he send it to you?” Her voice sounded high-pitched and squeaky.

Simeon’s face tightened. He averted his eyes. Dakota moved to the edge of the chair. The fuzzy feeling in her head thickened. He rounded his desk and opened a drawer. He pulled an old cassette recorder out and set the contraption on the desk in front of her.

"What is this about?" She looked around expecting to see balloons or a clown. This had to be some kind of joke, but Simeon wasn't smiling.

She shifted in her chair to get closer to the desk. The grim look in Simeon's eyes pleaded for understanding. Her thoughts cleared, like someone finally lifted the curtain exposing the stage. She shot out of the chair. "Are you telling me Brian is breaking up with me by way of you? What did he do, send you a text message to tell me we're through?" She chuckled hard.

"Please sit down, Dakota." Simeon rubbed her shoulder. "He sent me a tape that he wants you to listen to. He said he wanted to tell you the other night, but your call was disconnected."

"We haven't been able to have a decent conversation in months. He's in some remote area."

"He didn't want you to be alone when you heard what he had to say. He thought this would be a better way. But if you prefer, I can leave the room."

"No, please stay. I'm already humiliated, so what does it matter now? Let's call your assistant in too and anybody else who might like to witness the most embarrassing thing in my life since I tripped across the stage at my high school graduation." She started for the door, but Simeon pulled her back.

"Are you going to be okay?"

She sighed and motioned for Simeon to sit.

He popped a beat-up cassette tape into the recorder that was just as ancient, then looked over at her.

"This was the only thing he could find to record his message."

"Have you listened to the tape, yet?"

"No. He sent instructions on how he wanted this done. I shouldn't be in here listening to this either. You know how meticulous Brian is."

"Not meticulous enough to do this in person, but if you leave me alone, I'm going to scream like a banshee." She huffed and flopped back in the chair.

After nodding, Simeon started the tape. Brian cleared his throat several times. "Dakota, I know this is a horrible way to communicate something so important, but I had no other choice. I've been trying to tell you this for weeks." He paused. "I've accepted another mission assignment. In Central America this time. I'm leaving Haiti in two days. I don't expect you to understand, but I have to do this. The need is so great. I really care about you. More than I thought I could care about anyone. But you deserve more than I can offer." His voice dropped. "I'm not husband material. I think I always knew that and hoped I could change for you. But I can't change over thirty years of dysfunction. Go on with your life. Our paths might cross sometime in the future."

Dakota looked over at her brother-in-law. His head was down, studying the crease in his slacks.

"Please find it in your heart to forgive me for telling you this way and…and for leaving." The tape ended and the only sound was a whooshing like a big wind. No "goodbye". No "I'll miss you." No "I love you". Nothing. Pretty much the same way she felt. This had been coming for months, like locusts returning to a field.

She should be more upset. Throwing something across the room or kicking the desk might have been an appropriate response, but she didn't feel emotional. Maybe she'd let him down by not being supportive enough of his philanthropic efforts. Had Brian been upset as he recorded the message? Did he worry that his farewell might make her sad? He was too pragmatic to really care about such things. He saw the world as one big picture instead of realizing everyone had an individual snapshot.

Dakota straightened her legs in front of her, resting the tips of her boots on the base of Simeon's desk. They sat in silence for several minutes. She drummed her fingers against the chair while waiting for the tears or the aching in her chest.

"Has he found someone else?" she asked.

"I don't think he has. He's honest, he would have said so. I think he's crazy about you. He's just not the kind of guy who can stay put for long."

"You're taking up for your brother. You know this is wrong." She pointed her index finger at him.

He shook his head. "I'm not saying this is right. If he were here, I'd pop him upside his head. I just want you to be fine with the way this turned out."

"I'm going to leave now." She stared at the ceiling.

"You're sure you're okay?" He embraced her.

She bit her lip, contemplating her reply. She should be in tears. The hollowness in her chest wasn't because of Brian's message. She should have been brave enough to do the same thing months ago, while they could still use the phones like normal people. But she was a coward. She'd planned the same conversation when he came home. Anything was better than sending a Dear John letter. She lifted her hair off her neck.

"We were drifting apart. So this isn't a surprise. Even if I don't approve of his method, I'm glad he finally pulled the Band-Aid off. I feel like I can breathe now."

"Do you want to take the tape? It's yours."

She paused and gave him her full attention. "No. I don't need a reminder. I got the gist of what he wanted to say. Why don't you keep it? If he ever comes back to Bristol, give the damn thing to him."

He nodded. "I'll keep it in case you change your mind."

"Who else knows about this, Simeon?"

"No one. I haven't even told your sister. This is your story to tell."

"Your brother is a jerk. But I won't hold that against you." She kissed his cheek and left the office.

Chapter Four

The door to Simeon's office opened and Dakota walked out first. Instead of the big, bright smile she wore going in, her mouth was pinched tight.

Bishop knew enough not to ask questions. With the unhappy look on her face, she obviously didn't want to talk. If she wanted a ride, he'd take her where she needed to go. Nothing more. This one he had to leave alone. Her beauty was undeniable not sewn on, glued in, or baked on. A lot of good that would do him now since she was off limits. He shoved his hands in his pockets.

Simeon draped his arm over her shoulder and gave her a reassuring hug. "Bishop is going to take you home. I hope you don't mind, but he's doing this for me so I can get to a meeting."

"I can walk back to the bookstore." All the animation was gone from her voice. What could have happened in those few minutes in Simeon's office to short circuit the laughter he'd seen in her eyes?

"Let Bishop take you home, Dakota. I don't want you to be alone right now."

"Simeon, I'm fine. Really, I am. I don't like being away from the bookstore."

"Take some time," Simeon persisted. "Go home."

"Okay. If you insist."

Bishop held the outer door open. Dakota walked in front of him, leaving the scent of roses in her wake.

She gave Simeon a two-fingered wave before proceeding to the elevator. Bishop wanted to support her elbow, but decided against touching her. She appeared fragile and ready to flee. Her boots squeaked against the tile floor.

While they waited for the elevator, she rocked back and forth.

"Can I carry your backpack for you?" He wanted to assist her somehow.

"No. This is really my pocketbook. So I better handle it." She adjusted the bag on her shoulders and tightened the straps. "I'm sure you don't want to be seen carrying my purse."

"I'd carry you if that's what you needed. I don't care what people think."

"I'm okay." She stepped into the elevator and backed into a corner Bishop pushed the button for the lobby.

"Bad news, huh?"

She glanced at the ceiling of the elevator while tracing her tongue over her lips. He couldn't look away. Her gesture wasn't sexual, but it stirred him, as if she'd looked him in the eyes and dared him to watch her.

"Expected news." She finally looked at him. "Look, I know Simeon was being nice, but I really don't need a ride home. I'm fine. You can go do something more important."

"I'm sorry, but a promise is a promise." He led her out to the parking garage. After she was settled in the car, he closed the door, and walked to the driver side. Usually, troubled women sent him sprinting. But something about her vulnerability made him want to help. Be supportive. She was like magnet, pulling him closer.

"I live on Pocahontas Avenue.

"I know. Simeon gave me the address."

"How did you get stuck with taxi duty?"

"Not stuck. I volunteered. Simeon was in a pinch. I wanted to help him." He shrugged, hoping she wouldn't read anything more into his comment.

"Here I thought you were helping a damsel in distress." Her voice softened.

"Don't get it twisted. I'm where I want to be."

"I see. I could take that several ways." She managed a smile.

"Let me clarify for you. You look like you could use a friend right now. I'm being your friend." He glanced at her legs, but quickly returned his attention to the road. Good thing she didn't live far. The sooner he delivered her home, the better. He wasn't use to having women as chums, pals, or buddies.

"Oh, what about my car? I left it parked at Harper Enterprise." She glanced out the rear window as if she expected to see her vehicle following them.

"Don't worry." I'll make sure you get your vehicle back." He assured her.

She readjusted in the seat. "Do you mind if we stop and get a cup of coffee? I don't usually drink caffeine this late in the day, but I really need a jolt.

There's a little coffee shop on the next corner." She pointed.

"Sure. No problem." He slowed the car, then parallel parked into the open spot.

Bishop escorted her inside the store. The smell of espresso welcomed them. After placing their orders for two large mocha lattes, Bishop reached for his wallet.

"This is my treat. I can't expect you to drive me home and buy me coffee. I think you've endured enough for one day."

She pulled her purse off her shoulder and opened the zipper. He placed his hand on top of the bag to stop her. "I can't let you pay. I've got this. Why don't you get us a seat? I'll bring the drinks over."

She meandered through the maze of tables to one near the window. Her colorful boots were the only thing cheery about her now. The twinkle in her eyes from earlier had disappeared, along with her ready smile. She unraveled the long yellow scarf around her neck and draped it on the back of the chair.

With their orders in hand, Bishop made his way to the table. Dakota had her chin propped in the palm of her hand and gazed out the window.

He slid the cup in front of her. "Here you go. It looks like you could use a pick-me-up."

"Thank you. This is very nice of you." She held the cup between her hands. "Tonight is going to be cold." She could have been talking to anyone because she wasn't looking at him.

"You don't have to make small talk for me. It's obvious you don't feel like chatting."

"That's not true. I do feel like talking. I feel like screaming."

"Then go ahead. Let loose."

She looked around and shook her head. "I don't think so. Not here."

"Okay, we'll do things your way. Yes, the temperature is dropping. But that's okay, right?"

She faced him. "Cold is good. I will have an excuse to hibernate without having to explain my whereabouts. No one expects too much when the weather gets chilly."

"You sound like you want to go into hiding."

"I just want to be alone with my thoughts for a while." She looked into his eyes. "Have you ever started your day one way and then something happens to turn everything upside down?"

"Yes. That happens to everybody at least once." He nodded.

"Yeah, but it stinks."

"After a good night's sleep, whatever happened is never as bad as you thought."

Without replying, she smirked.

"Would you like to talk about what happened back there?"

"We are talking about it." She took a sip of coffee.

The late afternoon sun fell across her golden-colored skin, illuminating her even complexion. He wanted to run his finger along her jawline to see if she was as soft as she looked. The contrast between her smooth skin and her naturally curly hair made her look unique. Her large brown eyes searched his face. He could see pain behind her long dark lashes. Why was he just noticing her today?

"Tell me again how many times we've met."

"We were never formally introduced. But I've seen you at every party or public meeting held by Harper Enterprise over the last year. You're working on the community center aren't you?"

"I am. But I can't believe I never noticed you before."

"You know if you say that too often. it becomes an insult."

"Huh. I didn't intend that. I'm mad at myself. I usually notice all attractive women."

"I'll make a note of that." She looked out the window, dismissing him.

Dakota had spunk, and he liked women with spunk.

Chapter Five

Bishop hopped off the elevator in the lobby with a flair of freedom that he hadn't felt in weeks. He'd nailed it. The project at Harper Enterprise was on target. After multiple meetings, the community center should open on schedule and under budget. Simeon Harper was pleased with Bishop's work, which meant an extra bonus for his company. More money meant more pleasure. Maybe he'd take a dark haired beauty to Atlantic City for an extended stay.

Playing chauffeur last week had added brownie points to his Harper Enterprise bank. It also turned him on to a hidden treasure right here in Bristol: Dakota Conroy.

He stepped outside into the chilled October air to search the street for his sister. She should have been here to pick him up at three like they'd agreed. He pulled the collar of his suit jacket up to block the wind from his ears and bearded chin.

Tonight he'd celebrate his small victory with his sister and her lazy husband before checking his contact list for someone to warm his bed. Dad would be proud of him. Bishop was wealthy, single, and had a bevy of beautiful women willing to do his bidding.

He spotted his car at the stoplight. From the short distance, he could see Adanna's large, bright smile. The light changed and she pulled through the intersection and stopped in front of him. She put the car in park and hopped out.

"You drive. You know I hate driving in this congestion." She slid into the passenger seat and buckled her seat belt before he could comment. He placed his briefcase in the backseat and sat behind the wheel. His sister had only been driving a few months, so he understood her anxiety.

"You and Dennis need to buy your own car. I don't like being without my wheels," he said.

"Yeah, we will. But money is tight right now. How did your meeting go?"

He merged into the noonday traffic and tried to keep his face emotionless when he looked at her, but the heavy anxiety reflected in her eyes didn't warrant teasing.

"Better than I expected. We're on schedule and under budget. That means the performance factor in the contract kicks in. We're even working on other projects. It looks like I'll be spending more time in Bristol." He checked the rearview mirror before changing lanes.

"That's great." She clasped her hands together. "This is a happy day for us."

"What do you mean us?"

"Don't tease me, Bishop. You promised if you got the bonus and Dennis finished school, you'd lend us the money to buy the house."

He nodded. "How is your husband? Is he in school today?"

"He is in the library studying right now. One more month and he'll finish. Another engineer in the family."

"Where is the baby?" He lifted his eyebrow. "I hope you didn't leave him with Dennis while he's trying to study."

The bright smile Adanna gave her brother melted his heart. He wanted the very best for his only sister. And if she loved Dennis as much as she professed, he'd do everything he could to help the newlyweds. He'd tried to bury his anger that Dennis had impregnated his sister before he married her. Too bad she didn't get to have those wild years before settling down. His twenties were spent in a blur of women and parties. And it looked like his thirties would be the same.

"No, silly. DJ is with Dennis' mother. She wanted to spend some time with him. I'll pick him up later today." She paused for a moment. "Sharon showed up at my place today."

He chomped down on his jaw. "What did she want?"

"You."

"What did she say?" His tone was stern now.

Adanna huffed and rolled her eyes. "What she always says. 'Where's Bishop? Why isn't he returning my calls?' She thinks I'm not giving you the messages."

"Dammit. Sharon knows we're done. I made that very clear."

"Evidently not."

"She hears what she wants to hear. I even changed my cell phone number to get away from that hassling woman. That's why we're not together anymore. I'll talk with her again, and the next time she comes over, don't answer the door."

"How about you get me out of the middle of this mess? You know if you had a real girlfriend you wouldn't have these problems."

They rode in silence for several minutes. Adanna was stewing about something else and he decided to wait until she was ready to share it.

"Do you think Mom will ever forgive me?" Her voice dropped. Whenever the topic of her hurried marriage came up, she grew sad.

"What does it matter? If you're happy, that's what counts. Forgive yourself first, Adanna. Once Dennis gets a good job and can take care of you and DJ, I'm sure Mom and Dad will accept him into the family."

"Why is she so hard on me? She didn't say anything to you about your last girlfriend and it was obvious all she wanted was your money. Walking around asking how much everything cost."

"Mom never met her, and I didn't keep her around too long. But she was fun while she lasted. Mom knows I'm not thinking about settling down. She expects us boys to act like Dad and sow our wild oats. She just wants us to do it before we're married. And that's exactly what I plan to do."

"Don't you get lonely?"

"Who has time for that? I have plenty of women friends to keep me company."

"You need to leave those flashy gold-diggers alone. You need someone who cares about you and not your bank account. I'm sure that's why Sharon is still lurking around."

"I'm doing just fine, thank you. I know my choice of women doesn't meet your standards. I'm not looking to settle down, yet. Give me ten more years."

"Everything about you shrieks, 'Come look at all the material stuff I have!' Until you change that, all you're going to attract are good-looking women that don't really care about you."

"You think I care what women think of me? I just want their company for a while. When I get bored or they become boring, that's my signal to move on.

Adanna settled back in the seat. "You are turning thirty-three in a few months. I'll make it my responsibility to find you a wife. Maybe then we can get Mom and Dad to fly in for the wedding."

"I'll leave that to you and Dennis, marriage sounds boring to me."

§§§

Dakota sat at her kitchen table overlooking her small backyard. The leaves from the oak tree fell like rain in a steady pattern, blanketing the yard in a carpet of yellows and reds.

Jennifer couldn't hold down the bookstore by herself much longer. She was probably staging a mutinyalready.

This week felt pretty much like last week, only now she didn't have to wait on a call from Brian. It wasn't coming. For the last several days, she'd tried to determine who was the bigger coward, him or her. At least he'd made a move. She'd ignored her feelings hoping something would change, even though she knew nothing would.

The bowl of soggy corn flakes sitting in front of her was about as appealing as the dried leaves in the yard. Sooner or later she'd need to pull herself out of this blue funk and get back to life. She hadn't stepped foot in the bookstore in a week. Unsure what was most hurtful, the idea that Brian broke up with her, or the way he chose to end their relationship. Her heart felt like it had been hallowed out and filled with rocks. Jennifer must've thought she was nuts. Pretty soon, the world would come looking for her.

The phone rang. Instead of bounding for it like she'd done for over a year, expecting Brian to call, she settled back in the chair. The message light had started blinking two days ago, but she refused to check the messages for fear Brian might call. She had no idea what she'd say to him. Thank you for doing what I couldn't. You should have told me, yourself.

"Get up, Dakota. Get up." She pushed the cereal around the bowl before dumping it into the sink. One large brown glob slid into the drain.

The doorbell rang before she could climb the stairs. She went to the door and leveled her eye against the peep hole. Bishop Contee stood on her stoop, looking damn delicious. She turned away and slid below the viewer.

"Now what?" she whispered as she eased away from the door.

"I hear you by the door, so you can't pretend you're not home." There was laughter in his voice.

Through the door, she responded, "I'm not really dressed for company. What do you want?"

"To see you."

"Can you come back some other time?"

"I could, but since I'm here and you're here, we can do this now. I'm not going anywhere until I see you."

She looked through the hole at him again. With his hands at his side and his eyes covered by dark sunglasses he looked like a special agent. But why was he here? She looked down at her baggy sweatpants, tank top, fluffy pink slippers and moaned.

With a grunt, she opened the door. The trench coat and the suit made him look too serious to be standing at her front door.

"Can I come in?" His deep, sexy voice made saying no impossible.

She stepped aside and allowed him to enter. After she closed the door, she leaned her back against it. His eyes landed on the dinner plate from the night before still parked on the coffee table, and the stack of books cluttering the sofa. She closed her eyes, wishing she could clear the mess with a blink.

"Why are you here?"

"Last week when I dropped you off, you were unhappy. I decided to just check on you. I went by your bookstore yesterday. Your assistant said you weren't there. This morning when she said the same thing, I thought I'd come here."

"That's nice of you." She rushed to the chair and buried a pair of socks in the cushion. "I'm fine. I just decided to take a little time for me."

"Do you mind if I sit?" Bishop looked around the room.

"You're going to be here a while, huh?"

"You don't mind, do you?" His eyes sparkled with mischief.

She hesitated a moment. A man hadn't been in her house in over a year. Seeing him in the small confines of her messy living room made her schoolgirl giddy.

"Okay, have a seat." She moved the books to the table. He sat on the edge of the sofa without taking his eyes off her.

"How are you doing?" He looked her over like he was inspecting a piece of meat.

"Better." She sat across the room.

"I hope you don't mind me dropping by."

"What, just in case I'm suicidal?" She couldn't help being snippy. Now he cared? He should've remembered sitting next to her at the public meeting. It was only a year ago.

"No. That's not why I came by. You left your scarf in my car and I wanted to return it." He pulled a huge bright ball from his trench coat pocket and held it out to her.

She reached for her scarf and wrapped the length around her neck. "You could have left it with Simeon's assistant."

"I've come at a bad time?" He looked around the room.

"Yeah. Let's go with that."

"Are you always that outspoken?" He rubbed his hands together while nodding.

"Evidently not. If I had been, I would have freed myself from a bad situation a year ago."

He lifted an eyebrow.

"My boyfriend broke up with me."

"I see." His eyes twinkled and he smiled just a bit. "So that's the reason for the long face?"

"You're a quick study."

"Everything happens for a reason."

"I'll remember that." She shifted in the chair.

"If you need a listening ear, I'm here for you."

"There isn't much to say. Nothing interesting, anyway." She jumped up. "Can I offer you a cup of coffee?"

"No." He stood. "I have to get to the office. But I'd like to take you to dinner tonight to lift your spirits."

She looked down at her attire. "Thanks, but no."

"Maybe another time, then."

"Yeah, we'll see."

At the door, she thanked him again for the scarf and gently closed the door behind him.

The phone rang again. Her stomach knotted. She'd planned a whole speech for Brian, but now the words wouldn't come together in her head. The sharp edges of anger had dulled, but the thought of talking to him was taxing. She slogged to the counter and picked up the receiver.

"Dakota?" Asa asked.

"Whew! I'm glad it's you and not—never mind."

"I've called the store. Jennifer said you haven't been there in days. Are you okay?" The concern in her voice made Dakota wince. The last thing her sister needed was to worry about her.

"I'm fine. Really, I am."

"What is going on?" Asa stressed each syllable.

"I decided to take a few days off. I needed time to think."

"Stop lying to me. You love that store. When you need a break, you go sit with the books."

Dakota put her elbows on the table. "Brian sent me a Dear John tape."

"What's that?"

"He broke up with me, Asa. He sent a message for Simeon to play for me. How corny is that?"

"Oh no. When?"

"A few days ago. Don't start worrying about me. I'm fine. Today is the last day of my pity party." She almost mentioned Bishop, but decided she was making more of him than necessary. He only offered to take her to dinner, not to meet his mother. "Hey, Asa, would you call me pretty?"

"Okay. Pretty."

"No, I mean, why do men seem to overlook me? Brian left me twice, once in high school and again this month. I can sit next to a man in a meeting and he never even notices me. For the last year, I've been the unmarried maiden and that went out of style at the turn of the century."

"Look, I'm going to pack up the baby. We should be there shortly."

"No, Asa. Not today. I'm doing okay. I'm just angry he dumped me so callously and I'm mad at myself for being upset. My stomach churns every time I hear that tape playing in my head."

"Don't do that, Dakota. Don't beat yourself up wondering about things that you can't get the answers to. Brian is a grown man. He'll make out just fine," she paused. "Now, do you want me to come over there and keep you company?"

"No. You're right. You're absolutely right. I need to make up for lost time. I'm crawling out of this hole. I bounce back pretty quickly. As a matter of fact, I think it's time I've had some fun. A lot of fun," she said.

"Tell you what. Come to dinner here tomorrow night. Simeon has invited a few people over. Come join us. You can play with Mia."

"I won't promise, but I'll try. You know Mim used to say my promises were like pie crust—easily broken. So if I don't show up, don't hold my absence against me."

"I will." Asa laughed and hung up.

Dakota charged up the stairs and dressed in her favorite jeans. At the front door she pulled her coat off the hook, grabbed her backpack, and headed out. Her bright yellow car was parked out front, but she opted to walk the mile to the bookstore. The fresh crisp air could only make her feel better.

She headed to Mulberry Avenue toward the center of town. It was late enough in the morning that rush hour congestion was gone.

The shops along the street were going through a major renovation. Ever since Simeon began building the community center, the store owners had started sprucing up their businesses.

She glanced across the street at the brightly colored trim on several buildings, including the antique shop and the jewelry store. Each one had chosen a different pastel color. The pinks, greens, and yellows made her think of a small southern community. Now was the time to do something to the bookstore. The drab colors of Bookends' exterior weren't inviting.

Business had slowed. A makeover might bring her loyal customers back into the store. At least sprucing up the place would give her something to do with the empty hours in her day. The smell of fresh bread drew her into the bakery three doors from the bookstore. Behind the counter was a young girl she didn't recognize, so instead of chatting, she purchased a dozen glazed donuts and hurried out.

Dakota pushed open the door to the bookstore with her hip. "Good morning, Jennifer," she greeted her assistant.

Well, it's about time. If you didn't show up here today, I was going to bring every book in this store right over to your house."

"Good morning to you, too," Dakota teased. "I see I was missed." She placed the box of donuts on the far end of the counter before removing her coat. "I brought a peace offering. Why don't you have something sweet? It might help improve your mood."

"I don't need help with my mood. What I need is a good night's sleep. Brownie snored all night. I had to keep jabbing him in the side." Jennifer complained about her husband every day. She didn't know how lucky she was to have him to cuddle up with every night.

"Leave that man alone. He works hard. He should be able to sleep any way he wants." Dakota picked up her backpack and headed to her office. "At least you have someone to cozy up to at night."

Dakota flopped behind her desk and turned on the computer. Feeling better simply because one of the best looking men she'd seen in months asked her out, was silly. But she couldn't suppress the bubbly feeling. She wasn't Bishop's type, but sitting across a table from him would have been thrilling. Maybe that was the signal she needed to take control of her life.

After placing a few orders, she searched the Internet for renovation ideas. First the store, then herself.

The loud ringing of her personal line interrupted her search.

"Bookends," she said into the receiver.

"Dakota, its Melissa." Her sister's familiar voice came across the line. "I've called several times. Did you get any of my messages?"

"I've been really busy. I'm sorry. How are things in San Francisco? How's Darius?"

"Don't ask me about him."

"Are you mad at him again? Was he snoring last night, too?"

"Snoring? What are you talking about?" Melissa's casual tone changed to her proper schoolteacher voice.

"Nothing. It's just an ongoing joke between Jennifer and me. What's up with hubby?"

"I'd rather not talk about him right now." Her voice cracked. "I might be coming that way in a few weeks for Thanksgiving."

"Are you okay? Are you crying?" Dakota sat up straighter in her chair. Melissa never cried. Even at their parents' funeral, she hadn't shed a single tear. Melissa was the stoic one, busy being the big sister in control.

"No, I'm not crying. Look, let me call you back in a day or two. By then, I should know if I'm coming or not."

"Don't you want to stay with Asa? You know my housekeeping doesn't meet with your standards."

The last thing I want is to be around two love birds, kissing and screwing like rabbits."

"Oh, then you'll definitely want to stay with me."

Chapter Six

Dakota looked in her closet for something to wear to her sister's dinner party. She pushed aside the pale yellow dress. The color didn't speak to her. Even though Asa made the dinner sound casual, Dakota knew better. Everything Simeon and Asa did was on a grand scale.

The deep purple dress with the low-cut V-neck might be good. She pressed it against her shoulders and stared at her reflection in the mirror. The bold color lifted her spirits. Now was the best time to say goodbye to the gloomy Dakota. She refused to allow Brian to control another moment of her life.

"This should work." She twirled around and grinned.

She pulled the dress over her head, pushed her arms into the long sleeves, and tied the sash on her right hip. Her breasts pushed against the thin fabric. She stood on her toes to decide which heel height would give her that glamorous feeling she needed tonight. In her closet, she found the three inch sparkling silver pumps she adored. After slipping them on, she clicked her heels together.

"Have a good time. Have a good time. Have a good time," she chanted.

Brian's picture on her nightstand caught her eye. She used to think his solemn smile meant he worried about righting the wrongs in the world. Now she knew the look meant he needed to get away from her and the commitment she represented.

After removing the back from the small wooden frame and pulling his picture out, she looked around the room, unsure of what to do with the photograph. Ripping it would have been easy, but they had unfinished business. He owed her an explanation for his behavior. She turned the pictured face down on the dresser.

After a quick fluff of her loose curls, she applied a nude lip gloss and headed out the door.

As she pulled into the circular drive in front of Simeon's and Asa's house, she noticed all the cars. There were at least ten of them lining the drive. Asa's idea of a small get- together made her smile.

She spotted Bishop's blue Lexus just beyond the door and brushed her finger across the base of her chin. She didn't need to be in his company again. Thoughts of him popped in and out of her head at the weirdest times, while showering, or watching game shows. The last thing she needed was a playboy occupying her thoughts. Bishop changed women like Mother Nature changed the weather. At the Christmas party he was with a blond, at the summer picnic he was with a tall brunette. Tonight, there could be a redhead glued to his lips.

Dakota hurried to the door. She was about to have some fun. Her stomach somersaulted as she planned her future and rebirth. It was time to shake up her life. Tomorrow she'd call up her girlfriends to catch up on all the things she'd missed while she'd been hibernating. Why she'd been willing to play this miserable role for Brian still puzzled her. But now, she wanted no part of that. She should have accepted Bishop's offer for dinner. He could be a nice distraction, a way to get back into the dating game, to reactivate her dating stamina. There was no way she could ever take Bishop seriously, so there was no way she could get hurt.

After a year of being alone, just the thought of a risky relationship with a gorgeous man made her body warm. Bishop looked good. He had two arms, two legs, a strong, lean body and most of all, he was here, not stuck in a remote location. She'd been too harsh on him yesterday. If she could get a minute alone with him without whatever beauty he had clinging to him tonight, she might offer him an apology for her behavior.

She shook her head. Before she could ring the bell, Asa opened the door and flung her arms around her neck.

"I'm so glad you came. I've been looking out the window all evening for you."

Dakota peeped around Asa, trying to detect the size of the crowd. "How many guests are you expecting tonight? I thought you said this was a small party."

"Oh girl, get in here. We only invited a few people from Harper Enterprise and a few of my favorite customers. Nothing fancy." Asa grabbed her arm and pulled her inside. "Besides, you needed to get out of the house and have some fun."

Dakota dropped her backpack at the door. "I've actually gone back to work, thank you very much."

Asa eyed her bag, then rolled her eyes to the ceiling. "When are you going to get something more sophisticated?"

"What's wrong with my backpack? That bag has lots of compartments and it didn't cost a small fortune."

"Well, someone has a birthday soon. I know what to get you now." Asa grinned. Dakota kissed her cheek. "Now where is my niece? I need some hugs."

"I hope you're ready for drool. Come on back. We're all in the game room."

Dakota followed her sister. She could hear cheerful chatter. As they rounded the corner to the huge room, she couldn't help but search the crowd for Bishop. She spotted him seated on the leather sectional. His large hands were wrapped around Mia while he bounced the baby on his knees. She chewed on her fist while giving him a wet grin.

Simeon broke away from a small gathering and approached. Dakota embraced her brother-in-law.

"How are you?" The extra squeeze he gave her was loaded with meaning.

She patted his forearm. "I'm fine. Everyone needs to stop asking me that question. Don't I look better today than the day I slogged out of your office?"

He pulled back and glanced at her from head to toe. "You look fabulous." He laughed.

"Have you heard any more from Brian?"

He exhaled, shifting his position and looking uncomfortable. "No."

"Do you think—"

"Dakota, forget about Brian. No matter what, you need to move on. As my sister, I'm telling you, this little stunt was the last straw. Move on." He emphasized his words.

He guided her by the elbow into the crowd, introducing her to his new Human Resources Manager, Marshall Hanks and his ultra-thin, former-model wife, Olivia. After greeting them, she made her way to the seat next to Bishop.

"Do you mind if I hold her a while? I haven't seen my sweet pea in weeks." She held out her arm and Mia leaned forward, trailing a stream of saliva.

"I don't think I could stop her if I wanted to." Bishop placed the baby in her lap.

The light touch of his arm as he passed the baby sent a jolt of excitement through her. Like a new girl in school, all her cute conversation starters escaped her thoughts. What could she say to the man who had women hanging from his arm any time he wanted?

"Are you stalking me? In the past few days, I've seen you at Simeon's office, my house, and now at my sister's party." Dakota swallowed. That's not what she intended to say. She wanted to sound witty and sophisticated. She held her niece's hand as Mia reached for her necklace.

"No, but don't give me any ideas."

"Let's see if your date agrees." Dakota looked around the room for the woman with the biggest breasts, narrowest waist, and longest lashes.

"As a matter of fact, I'm alone tonight. I was hoping you'd show up alone too."

"That's pretty much a sure bet, considering my circumstances."

"I shouldn't have phrased my statement that way."

She waved his comment away. "Don't worry. I'm over him. I'm unleashed on the world now. And if they knew what I know, they'd better run for cover. I'm taking no prisoners."

"Wow that sounds exciting." He rubbed his hands together.

"Oh, that's my intention." Dakota glanced down at Mia as the baby started to squirm.

"No fancy boots tonight?" he asked.

She grinned and stuck out her high-heeled foot. "I thought tonight I'd dress up a bit. Asa hates for me to wear boots when it's not raining, and certainly not to one of her dinner parties. I see you're still wearing the same attire."

His smile widened. "Different suit and different loafers."

"Yeah, different, but the same." Dakota surveyed the crowd. "Out of all the beautiful women in this room, why aren't you chasing one of them down?"

He broke into a hearty laugh that made Mia squeal, too. "What does that mean? You make me sound pretty desperate."

"Like my Mim said. If the shoe fits, wear it."

"Who is Mim? And why would she say that about me?"

It was her turn to laugh. "My grandmother. She had a saying for every occasion. Not just for you."

"She sounds like she was quite a person."

"She was pretty special. After our parents died, she held my sisters and me together, dishing out her wisdom in clichés." Dakota wiped the drool off the baby's chin with the bib tied around her neck.

He nodded. "You look radiant tonight." He smiled and instead of making baby sounds, Mia grinned at him. Judging from Mia's reaction to him, he might not be the bad playboy she'd pictured.

"You know, I can't remember the last time someone called me radiant. I know you're probably just being nice, but thanks just the same."

"I wouldn't make a comment I didn't mean." He tickled Mia under the chin, but looked at Dakota.

"You better be careful or she'll spit on you." Dakota wiped Mia's chin again.

"I'm not afraid of a little spit." His hand brushed hers as Dakota cuddled Mia. If only his touch could have lingered longer. Long enough for her to remember the feeling tonight while she lay alone in her bed, again.

"So where is your girlfriend, tonight?" Dakota held the baby up on her wobbling legs.

He directed his attention on her. "I don't have a girlfriend. I have lots of friends. Some of them are female. My life's not more complicated than that." He held out his left hand for her to examine. "I'm not married. I'm not into commitment. Permanent relationships work well for some people, but not for Contee men." His voice trailed off.

"What does that mean?"

He cleared his throat. "I have three brothers. We're all single and plan to stay that way. My father should have remained single, but my brothers and I have vowed to learn from our parents' experience."

"That sounds like a story."

"Oh, I've got a story alright. But not one I should share during a dinner party."

"Okay. Then tell me what you're doing in Bristol. Dressed like that, I'd think Bristol was too slow for you."

"It is. I live in Philly."

"I should have known." Dakota directed her attention back to her niece.

"Should have known what?" He sat forward and looked at her face.

"I can kinda tell. You look like you live life in the fast lane. The pool of available women in Bristol probably isn't big enough for you."

"I'll ignore that last comment, but I get the impression you're no slouch when it comes to enjoying life either. Besides, I'm sitting with a woman right now that puts any others in the pool to shame."

"Who, Mia?"

"Mia's aunt." The playfulness disappeared from his voice.

She tried to hide her smile, but couldn't. Teasing with him was enjoyable. But the serious turn in the conversation made her uneasy. Bishop was an Adonis—on any given day. And she felt like Cinderella dressed up for the ball. In her real world, she wore jeans, tank tops, and an unruly ponytail. After a year of celibacy, her body reacted to his declaration like he was the antidote for her lonely heart.

From the other side of the room, she saw Simeon run his hand along Asa's butt. Dakota turned away from the intimate gesture.

"Well, I used to take one step at a time, but now I've vowed to make up time."

"What does that mean?"

"I plan to sow some wild oats. I deserve to have some fun, and I plan to have as much fun as my two hands can hold."

"I'm intrigued. What do you have planned?"

His sensuous smile lit a desire in the pit of her stomach. Good thing her niece was planted in her lap or she might have climbed on his.

Simeon stood in the doorway. "Dinner is ready. We're eating on the patio, so come on." He waved everyone over.

"It's cold outside." Dakota glanced at her sleeveless dress and bare legs.

"The fire pit is nice and hot. You'll be warm," Simeon continued motioning everyone outside. "Besides, it's time for Clara to put Mia to bed." The au pair took Mia out of her arms. "Good night, sweet pea." Dakota kissed her niece's forehead.

"Do you mind if I sit with you tonight?" Bishop walked with her to the patio.

"I'd like that."

Her stomach rolled over.

He said, "I want to finish our conversation. You didn't answer my question."

"About how I live my life? Well let's say the future will be quite different than the past. I'm planning to have more fun. To live like I've never done before."

§§§

Dakota's declaration stirred every cell in his body. She might as well have waved her panties under his nose. From the moment she'd entered the room, Bishop had followed her movements. Her graceful walk, easy smile, and understated elegance were hard to ignore. The dress exposed her shapely legs and her lovely cleavage.

She passed the mirror as they made their way outside without stopping to check her hair or makeup. A woman who wasn't stuck on her appearance. Refreshing. The casual curve of her lips demonstrated she wasn't too excited about being there. He hoped her indifference would make her receptive to his charm, instead of being focused on the way he led his life.

On the patio, she plopped into a cushioned rattan chair as he made his way to the elegant buffet table. "I'll bring you a plate."

He couldn't look at anyone but her. Such a welcome surprise, her being there tonight. Since dropping by her house, he'd wondered when he'd have another opportunity to find out more about the exceptional beauty. Now, instead of spending the night trying to impress the boss, he would spend the night trying to impress Dakota.

Her smoky dark eyes surveyed the patio and landed on him. Heat climbed up his back when he caught her attention. He held her gaze for a moment, but those few seconds were enough to touch him like nothing had before.

The table was loaded with traditional barbeque food. The smell of grilled meat filled the air. Bishop grabbed two plates and filled them, before heading back in her direction.

"I wasn't sure what you might like, so I gave you choices." Bishop handed her a plate laden with brisket and steak along with a hot dog and a mound of salad.

She accepted the plate. "Thank you, Bishop. This is enough food for a truck driver." The sincere smile she gave him boosted his confidence.

Forward women were about as common to him as his ten pairs of Italian loafers. But the way Dakota dropped her head whenever he looked in her eyes said she wasn't one of them. Living a different life was easier to talk about than it was to follow through. As much as he tried to be different from his father by remaining single, there was an emptiness in the pit of his stomach that begged to be filled.

He took the seat across from her. "Whatever you don't eat, I'll take care of. If I'd piled all I wanted on my plate, I'd look like a pig."

"With all the food they've prepared, we all will need to eat like pigs tonight."

She set the plate on the glass table and cut the brisket. He watched her mouth as she spoke. Her lips were full. He tried to imagine what it would feel like to kiss her.

"I'm also thinking about making some other changes." She gave him an earnest look.

"Yeah. How did you put it? Your future life will be different from your past life?"

"Not only changes in my personal life. I mean my business, too. I'm thinking about remodeling my bookstore. I haven't done anything to the place in the last five years. The block going through a renaissance and I need to keep up or I'll be going out of business."

"What do you have in mind?"

"I haven't got a clue. But since my brother-in-law has the biggest construction company in the area, I don't need to, right?"

"Maybe I can stop by and give you some ideas."

"I couldn't ask you to do that. After chauffeuring me around last week, I think I've tortured you enough."

"I don't mind. Besides, I volunteered."

"You do a lot of volunteering don't you? Is that how you keep your steady supply of available women?" Her comment was accompanied with a smile, which took some of the sting out of the punch.

"Available supply? What does that mean?"

"Don't pretend you don't know that I mean. It would be disingenuous."

He swallowed. She knew more about him than he wanted to share. Did she think he was a womanizer? "I'm just enjoying life. I tell everyone where I stand. So there's no lying, cheating, or whining."

She chewed the meat and nodded. From the way she clenched her jaw, his remark had struck a chord with her and not necessarily a good one.

"I guess if you give me some tips or pointers, that couldn't hurt. If Simeon doesn't object, you've got yourself a deal." She stuck out her hand.

He gripped it and held on. "Deal."

They were still chatting as the guests began to leave. The soiled dishes had been picked up hours before. Now the only things on the table were their wine glasses.

"I better go. It's getting late." Dakota stood and ran her hand down the front of her dress.

Bishop jumped up. "Let me walk you to your car."

Her eyes widened, but she smiled. "Okay, let me say goodnight to Asa and Simeon."

Together they walked inside. After shaking Simeon's hand, Bishop waited while Dakota found her purse. With his hands buried deep in his pockets, he rehearsed a speech in his head to spend more time with her.

"Okay, I'm ready." She breezed past him and out the front door.

He closed the door and caught up to her. "I was serious when I asked you to dinner. So if I ask you again what will you say?"

She stopped and stared at him. "You mean you weren't asking me out because you felt sorry for me?"

"Why would I feel sorry for you?"

She bit her lip without replying.

"How about I take you for a drink tonight?"

"It's late." She looked at her watch. He reached for her hand.

"I want to spend more time with you."

She looked up at the night sky and then returned her gaze to him

"Follow me." She released his hand and hurried down the path.

"Where are we going?"

"To my place."

Chapter Seven

Dakota slid behind the steering wheel and buckled her seatbelt before exhaling. Her heart thumped so fast her hands shook as she started the car. Mim said loneliness made strange bedfellows, but just for one night, that was exactly what she wanted. She eased the car down the lane and onto the main street. Bishop was tall, lean, and more than capable of filling the empty spot in her heart for a few hours. She didn't want a commitment or promises for tomorrow. All she wanted was one glorious night to pretend she was worth having.

She checked the rearview mirror. He was still behind her. He hadn't changed his mind and taken the ramp to the interstate.

Her palms began to sweat as she gripped the steering wheel. "Calm down, Dakota. It's only sex. Like riding a bike, you didn't forget how." She checked the mirror again, half expecting him not to be there, but relieved that he was.

She pulled in front of her house and turned off the car. After a deep breath, she ran her clammy hands on her bare legs to keep from smearing perspiration on her silk dress.

The knock on the driver-side window startled her. She opened the door.

"I didn't mean to scare you. You are getting out of the car, aren't you?" He stood so close to her she could smell his cologne.

"Yes, of course." She grabbed her backpack and headed up the stairs.

Inside, she turned on the lights in the entryway before dropping her bag on the table.

"I know this might seem forward, but I can't wait another minute." He placed his hand behind her neck. The heat from his touch radiated throughout her body, waking every dormant cell. Calling her to life. He pulled her forward. His mouth covered hers. The warmth of his tongue enveloped her whole body. Their dueling tongues started slow, with such tenderness she melted against his rock-hard chest. Encircling his waist with her arms, she held on to him as if he were the only thing keeping her feet on the floor.

Like a sleeping giant, her body roared awake as his tongue slid deeper. Everything about Bishop was as good as she imagined.

His smell.

His taste.

His touch.

Him.

Blood rushed to her loins, heating her like nothing ever had before. She couldn't pull away from him if an earthquake struck Delaware and shook the house from its foundation.

He removed his jacket it landed at her feet without making a sound. After untying the sash at her waist, he pushed the dress away from her breasts. He kissed her neck. His short beard scratched her skin, arousing desire buried under layers of loneliness. He placed his mouth over her nipple and pulled it gently. A moan traveled from the pit of her stomach, up to her chest. She released it in one long sound that she thought would never end.

With the skill of a master craftsman, he helped her out of the dress and captured her other breast in a strong hand. She arched her back making it easier for him. Part of what she was feeling was only pent-up desire from a year of longing and wanting. But a bigger part of the emotion surging through her was all about Bishop. For tonight she wanted to pretend this was more than lust. She unzipped his pants and found his hardened shaft. She trailed her finger along his fullness in the tight confines of his boxers. Another moan filled the room. This time it was Bishop's. Two consulting adults could certainly enjoy each other without reprimand.

She pushed the thought away when he placed his finger inside her thong and drew the garment down her legs. She kicked off her heels and stepped out of her panties. He pressed her against the wall and kneeled to bury his head between her thighs, running his tongue along her nub. His precision made her body stiffen. Nothing had ever felt so exquisite in her life. If she never had sex again, this moment would be burned in her memory forever.

He lifted her into his arms and carried her upstairs. At the top of the landing, she pointed to her bedroom.

From the edge of the bed, she reached for the light on the nightstand. "Time for you to come out of these clothes. I have a no-clothes rules in here." She unbuttoned his shirt.

"We think alike." He kicked off his shoes.

She pushed his pants and boxers down his thick, strong legs and he stepped out of his clothing.

He lowered her down on the bed and planted kisses in the cleft of her breasts, across her stomach, and between her legs. His tongue slipped into her wet folds again, stroking her to life. When she invited him back to her place this was exactly what she wanted. She couldn't have imagined he would be so adept in satisfying her. He breathed life into places that had been asleep for a year. His tender touch almost brought her to tears.

The pressure in her core surged like a tsunami gathering strength to come on shore. She closed her eyes and surrendered to the power of each wave washing over her, first lifting her up off the bed, then pulling her back with such force she cried out his name.

For a full minute, she tried to catch her breath, refusing to open her eyes and allowing the ecstasy to vanish.

"Are you still with me?" His voice was soft against her ear.

"Just barely."

"I can do that again if you like."

She opened her eyes to look at him. In the dim light, his dark eyes were intense and penetrating.

"No. This time I do you." She pushed up.

"I don't have any condoms." She sat all the way up. "No condoms? How can a playboy not have a wallet full of protection?"

"Well, first of all I was going to dinner at the home of my business partner. I had no idea the night would end in a sex-fest." He cupped her breasts in the palms of his hands. "But I'm glad it did."

"Aren't you always prepared?" She positioned herself in front of him on her knees.

"Not well enough I see."

She sucked her teeth and climbed out of bed.

"Where are you going?"

"I've got to have one or two around here somewhere." She pulled open the drawer on the nightstand and pushed aside the papers and books. She slammed the drawer shut. "Nothing there."

He reached for her as she climbed across him and out of the bed. In the bathroom, she flipped on the light and opened the medicine cabinet, scanned it, then closed the door. In the bottom drawer of the vanity, she found two condoms stashed in the corner.

She caught a glimpse of her image in the mirror before leaving. She'd done exactly what she intended. She'd actually invited a man to her place and had her way with him. Until tonight the things Bishop had done to her body were only a fairytale. What a way to liberate herself from all that old baggage.

She took a deep breath and steadied her excitement. As soon as she got this need to liberate herself out of her system, she could return to real life, where dreams didn't always come true, she got her feeling hurt and good girls didn't chase men—no matter how good-looking.

The thought of Bishop as she crawled over him a moment ago made her smile. Maybe she'd send him flowers for being such a willing participant in her fantasy weekend. She turned off the light, but remained in the darkened room for a moment. The sensible side of her brain warned her to stay in the safety of the bathroom. The lonely side of her brain screamed to be held and loved, even if only for one night.

She walked back into the bedroom to find him positioned on his elbow staring in her direction.

"If they aren't dried out, this should last us a while." She held them up by the tips.

He removed the foil-wrapped condoms from her hand and pulled her down on top of him. With her in the cradle of his arm, he ripped one package open with his teeth. She helped him roll the sheath into place over his erection. He inched his hand along her thigh. The heat from his hand sent a spark of electricity through her body.

"I want you, Bishop." Her voice sounded strained. She spread her legs as he inserted his finger deep inside her.

"You've had me all night."

"I want all of you."

"How's this?" The pad of his index finger found that sensitive spot and rubbed with an expertise that lifted her hips off the bed. She reached for his manhood, pulling him forward.

"Now, Bishop. Now."

He climbed between her legs. With his head buried in the curve of her neck, he slid inside of her. Her body expanded to accept him. Dakota clamped her arms around him. She rotated her hips, allowing him to drive deeper. One-night-stand guilt should have dampened her pleasure, but tonight the opposite was true. Each thrust sent an explosion of pleasure through her body that erased a year of lonely nights. She wrapped her legs around Bishop's back to draw him deeper. Together, they reached a perfect rhythm. The sensation started where the tip of his rod touched her and radiated through her body slow and steady. She felt like she wanted to sing and cry all at once as her body shook. Every muscle constricted at once. A sound rose in her throat but was lost before she could vocalize it. Instead she hung onto Bishop and squeezed him with every ounce of strength she could muster.

§§§

The drive back to Philly in the predawn hours had passed in a blur as Bishop relived every perfect detail of their weekend. Spending two full days with Dakota had been pure bliss. They only got out of bed long enough to buy more condoms and takeout food. Her passion seemed insatiable, but before the sky lightened the bedroom on Monday morning she was sprawled across the bed like a rag doll.

The passionate goodbye kiss she had given him before he left still lingered on his lips. The hammer in his head warned him to slow down. Dakota should have been out of his head the minute he hit the interstate. But that was hours ago, now he was home and she was still stomping through his thoughts. Instead of selecting a shirt from his massive collection, he wanted another dose of Dakota. He pulled the Brioni striped dress shirt from the hanger along with a solid blue tie. A quick look in the mirror and he nodded approval.

He promised Dakota he'd be at her bookstore by ten and he was running late. Never before had it mattered what someone thought of him. If they didn't like him, then he moved on. But this time, he felt different. What Dakota thought, mattered. Traffic was thick, but he managed to find a parking space close enough to get to the store on time. As he opened the door, a bell chimed his arrival.

He expected to be greeted by a vivacious Dakota smile. Instead, an older woman stood behind the register. She was preoccupied with breaking open a roll of pennies. After several whacks, the paper tore, releasing the coins with a jingle.

"Hi, I have an appointment with Dakota this morning. Is she here?

She looked at home over the reading glasses nesting on the tip of her nose and huffed. "Let me get her for you, she's in the back."

"No, let me walk back and find her. I can look around and get some design ideas as I go. Is that okay?"

She shrugged. "Fine with me. This isn't my store. I just work here. She don't tell me nothing." She waved him away. "You can't miss her."

He'd have plenty of time to get ideas on any changes, so he walked straight to her office. As he'd dashed out of her door this morning, all he thought about was seeing her again. Thinking about anything other than Dakota was impossible.

Adjusting his gait, he slowed his approach. Hidden by the tall shelf, he watched her twirl a lock of thick hair around a finger. She studied the book in front of her. He didn't know how to categorize his feelings for her and for now, he didn't want to. Maybe not knowing. That way, nothing was required of him.

She put the book on the desk and leaned over a box full of more books. Her tight jeans hugged her round butt. The bright red top she wore rode up her narrow waist and exposed the smooth skin on her back. He tried to look away, but couldn't.

He shook his left leg until his arousal abated, then he cleared his throat.

"Oh, hey, Bishop. You're right on time." She stood up and yanked her top down with one hand while placing more books on her cluttered desk.

He kissed her on the mouth, claiming her tongue with the familiarity of a lover. He wanted more, but tried to be appropriate.

She wrapped her arms around his waist, pulling him close enough, him to smell her fresh clean scent. After a moment, she fingered his suit jacket.

He looked down, expecting to see his fly open. "What? What is it?"

"Take off your jacket. It's too much for the store. I would make you take off those slacks too, but I guess that wouldn't be nice of me in my place of business."

"I'll shuck mine if you shuck yours."

"Mmm, maybe later."

He laughed. "Is that a promise?"

She pretended to think about it. "It could be if you play your cards right. We'll see."

"Do you want to discuss this weekend? I'm still weak in the knees."

She placed her hand flat against his chest and pecked his cheek. "I think I heard you leave this morning. I guess I ought to thank you. You were exactly what I needed." She looked into his eyes for a moment as if she was trying to convey a message.

"Evidently, I needed you too." He kissed her again.

"Now let me show you around. We'll start in the front and work our way back here. I think I want to change what the customer sees when they walk in."

"You're right. I'm here on official business. I'll follow you." He stepped out of her way hoping to get another glimpse of her butt as she walked by him.

He watched her swish her hips through the aisles.

"When customers walk in, I want them to feel like they've entered a more modern bookstore. There needs to be more light in here. And I want books to welcome people the moment they come in. Maybe we can find something more contemporary to display them on too. I don't like the way the books are just shoved on the shelves now. Also, I think the bookshelves should run this way, not that way." She motioned with her hand, indicating shifting the shelves in the opposite direction. Her animation made her one of a kind. Very different from any of the other women he dated who took themselves too seriously.

"Whoa, Dakota. I'm trying to keep up with you here." He jotted notes onto his electronic pad.

She crossed her arms. "I'm sorry. Let me slow down. You can see I'm really excited about these changes. This morning when I walked in, it was as if I saw the bookstore for the first time. I don't know how I let the store get in this state. I must have gone through a period of time with blinders on."

He glanced around. "It's not that bad. You've got some good ideas."

They spent an hour going over the details. Bishop had to scribble quickly to keep up with her list of wants. His mind kept drifting back to the weekend, to the enjoyment they'd shared and the pleasure they'd taken in each other's bodies.

"Can we stop for a minute and get some coffee? I saw a pot in the back." He used his head to nod to the back of the shop.

"Sure. I'm sorry if I'm overwhelming you. Once I set my mind on something, I usually plow straight ahead. I'll try to slow down."

"I like your go-get em attitude. But even the best of us need a rest sometimes."

"Are we still talking about the store or have you slipped into a memory?"

"What do you think?" He tickled her under her chin.

He closed the cover on the tablet and followed her with a smile. She poured coffee into Styrofoam cups.

"Sugar and cream?" she asked.

"Black." He took the cup from her hand and watched as she poured cream and several heaping teaspoons of sugar into her coffee.

"You like your brew really sweet, don't you?"

"The sweeter the better." She held the cup between her palms.

"You look happier today."

"I am. I feel like I've been checking the mail every day waiting on a letter and finally getting a good report. And as you know, I had a marvelous weekend."

"I did too, even though I'm paying for all that activity now. I didn't have the stamina to work out this morning, and I'd do everything—and I mean everything all over again."

She put her cup to her lips and immediately took it away. "Me too."

"I'm not sure I know the real Dakota Conroy. The woman from this weekend and the woman in the coffee shop don't jive."

"I'm a mixture of both. I'm working through some stuff. As soon as I'm done, I'll return to normal, the girl who doesn't invite men back to her home for a wild weekend."

"I see." He scratched his chin.

"You don't have a problem with that, do you?" She searched his eyes. "For a playboy like you, I thought that would be right up your alley."

Under different circumstances, he would have grinned like he'd hit the lottery. But the tingle along his spine warned him this might not be good news. He was used to setting the guidelines for the relationship. Taking direction from someone else made him uneasy. He tried to swallow coffee past the lump in his throat. "No problem at all." Whatever was going on, they'd work something out.

Chapter Eight

Dakota watched Bishop's face cloud over. He took several sips of coffee without looking at her. Her casual attitude should have made him do cartwheels. Isn't that what players always wanted to hear? Sex without the shackles of relationships and meeting the parents?

His eyes raked over her. Coming from a man used to dating a different girl every day of the week, the treatment made her giddy.

"I think I have enough to get started. Let me put some designs together and get back with you." He put his cup down.

The urge to touch his face surged through her veins. Maybe she hadn't satisfied her need for human touch yet because all she could envision was running her fingers through his beard and making him purr with pleasure. Maybe her loneliness was playing tricks on her.

She wondered what demons chased him. Why he refused to settle down. She pushed the thought away. Her job wasn't to fix him or hold him up while he found his way. If they could have fun together, that was enough. That was all she wanted for now.

His vow to stay uncommitted indicated something or someone had screwed with his head, but she didn't want to be his counselor. Let some other woman rub his shoulders while he poured out his heart. She wasn't playing that role anymore, for anyone.

He shifted his weight. She looked around the shop hoping to find something else to show him.

A quick glance at his watch and he announced, "It's almost lunch time. How about we grab a sandwich at the shop down the street? We can talk through some of your suggestions."

Thrilled by the invitation to spend more time with him her heart raced. "Let me get my bag." She started toward her office, suppressing a squeal.

"You won't need it. I'm paying." He picked up his jacket and placed his hand on her elbow, guiding her to the front of the store. The heady surge of heat from his touch made her heart race. She didn't want to expect too much—this was only a game with him. Pretty soon he'd move on to some other woman waiting in the queue.

"You bought the coffee the other day," she protested. Keeping things simple between them was best.

"Dakota, let me clear the air. Any time I go out with a woman, I'm paying. That's just my nature."

She grabbed her coat from the hook and fastened the buttons without taking her eyes off him. "Are we going out?"

He opened the door to the bookstore. "We're going out."

"Oh, that was real cute." She swatted at him and missed on purpose. Just being with him for a few days made up for the year she'd wasted with Brian.

They walked down the block in silence. She tried to find some warmth in her jacket, but the wind cut through her like she was wearing cotton. She shivered.

"Are you cold? "

"I'd pull out mittens but I might look silly since it's only October."

He opened the door to the small deli, the heat enveloping them as they stepped inside. Her shoulders relaxed as her temperature neared normal.

At the counter, she ordered tuna on rye.

"I'll have the same. If it's good enough for her, it must be delicious." He paid for their order and then turned to her. "Letting me pay wasn't so bad. See you didn't have a spasm." He stuffed his wallet back into his pocket.

She wrinkled her nose. "If I never get to treat you, I imagine things between us will get boring after a while."

"You treated me this weekend. I ate all your hummus." He kissed her cheek. "And I'm never boring."

"I can vouch for that."

They took their seats.

She believed him. Every conversation they had still resided in her head. This morning she'd recalled bits and pieces to keep them fresh in her mind.

Their number was called and Bishop sauntered to the counter to pick up their order. With the tray positioned between them, she reached for her sandwich and chips. He took a bite from his sandwich. "You own a bookstore, what do you like to read?"

"Everything. But I really enjoy—" Heat rose in her cheeks.

"You're blushing. What do you read? Those sexy books?"

"No, but most people think I'm nuts. I like to read historical love letters."

"What is that?"

"Famous letters, like the ones Napoleon wrote to Josephine and Churchill wrote to his wife, Clementine. I like them all, historical and fictional ones."

He tilted his head. His eyes adopted a faraway look. Was he thinking she was a nut, or some old maid who filled her time with someone else's life?

"That's interesting. You'll have to read to me one day."

"Why, so you can laugh at me?"

"I don't think I'd ever laugh at you." Something in his eyes invited her in. There was a warm glint that allowed her to feel okay about her ridiculous passion.

"Do you wear suits every day?"

"Not every day. Seldom on Saturday, and only for church on Sunday." He smiled…or maybe it was a smirk.

She laughed. "You know what I mean. Every time I've seen you, you've had on a suit. Do you own any jeans or khakis? How about a pair of shorts?"

"Do you want to see my legs again?"

She lowered her head. "I was only asking a question. Not making a come on."

"I like when you flirt with me." He lifted an eyebrow. "Since the weather is a little cold for shorts, I promise I'll sport a pair just for you in April, or whenever the temperature starts to warm again."

She bit her sandwich. The idea that he might still be around in the spring warmed her soul. Under the table, she tapped her foot with joy.

"Okay, you've got yourself a date," She tamped down her joy. No use letting him see too much. If he'd knew he just made a mini commitment he'd probably tear out of the coffee shop.

"I was thinking about a date a lot sooner than the spring. Like maybe this weekend."

"This weekend?" She hesitated. He was asking exactly what she wanted, but what she least expected. "What, another weekend sequestered in my house?" Her heart pounded while she waited for his answer. Did he think she was a sex toy, not to be seen in public?

"Actually, I was thinking about something not quite as strenuous. There is a concert in Philly. I'd like to take you. You like music, don't you?"

A date.

A real date.

She sat back in her chair with her hands folded in her lap. Going out with Bishop would be fun, but not practical. The only thing they had in common was the ability to burn up the sheets. The weekend had been a fun expedition and a marvelous way to shake loose the cobwebs off her life, but she couldn't push a weekend beyond that. In the deep curve of his smile resided disappointment. And if she pushed too hard something bad was bound to happen.

"I think I do. Of course I do. It's just that…that…"

"You've got something else planned?" Bishop leaned closer to her, his tone was flat and there was disappointment in his eyes.

"I can't this weekend. Maybe another time."

"So what's going on between us, Dakota?" He leaned across the table, his nose almost touching hers.

"Nothing yet."

"What about our weekend? Do you want me to pretend nothing happen?"

She balled up the paper her sandwich was wrapped in and pushed away from the table. "I better get back to the store."

He hopped up, taking their trash to the depository in the corner. "I'll give you a call tomorrow to discuss designs."

Outside, he gave her an informal embrace. His beard rubbed across her chin. The gesture was too stiff for people who had just shared each other with the wild abandonment of rabbits. She couldn't answer his question. It was just supposed to be fun, a bridge between Brian and her new world. But the feeling in her gut told her what they shared was more than a rumble in the sheets.

She didn't want to let go of him. The mournful nagging in the pit of her stomach made her drop her arms. If he intended to dismiss her, she didn't need to see the look in his eyes. If she learned nothing else in the last year, she'd learned to expect nothing, and save herself the heartache.

As he walked to his car, she eyed his strong shoulders. Even in his custom-made suit, she could see his strength. He gave her a quick wave before getting in his car.

She clenched her fist and headed back to
the bookstore. "Idiot. You should have said 'yes',"
she said under her breath.

95

Chapter Nine

If two days of pure fantasy proved anything, it proved her head was hard and her heart was soft. She wanted Bishop Contee like Juliet wanted Romeo. She wanted him to be her soul mate, if she believed in such things. But, she refused to be so gullible the next time around. Love like that only existed in the pages of the love letters she read, not in real life. She tightened her light jacket around her neck as she made her way down the street. Maybe she should wait a few months or years before even considering dating again to make sure she knew what she wanted. Or what she didn't want. Bishop wasn't the one. He actually said so himself. His little speech about staying unattached was like a warning flare. She wouldn't be foolish enough again to think she could turn a man around or make him want something he was hell bent on getting away from.

"What was that all about?" Jennifer asked as she walked into the bookstore.

"I'm thinking of re-doing the shop. The place needs a facelift, don't you think?"

"You know what I'm talking about. The way you were going on and on with that guy. I could tell it didn't have nothing to do with the shop. What about Brian?"

"He's history." Dakota hung her coat on the hook.

"I'm glad you finally recognized that." Jennifer stuffed a twenty-dollar bill under the register tray and slammed the drawer.

"You're saying you knew?" Dakota's chest constricted.

"Honey, when a man leaves his woman for a year and Uncle Sam didn't make him, the relationship is over," Jennifer clucked her tongue like a mother schooling a child.

"So, am I the laughing stock of the town?"

"No. Most people assumed you two broke up and that's why he left. The rest of us think you're just too nice."

"I see." She paused. "Anyway, Bishop is going to work on the store. Nothing more." She made her way to her office and closed the door. So much had happened in the last two weeks she couldn't keep everything straight. In her chair, she turned on the computer and found the pictures she had been saving, the plans for the party she'd expected to throw for Brian upon his return. She deleted them one at a time, banging the computer key with almost enough force to break the keyboard. Then she picked up the phone and dialed Harper Enterprise.

"Catherine, this is Dakota Conroy. I need to get in touch with Bishop…Bishop Contee. Can you put me through to his office, please?"

"Sure, Dakota. Hold on a moment."

The connection took longer than she expected. She almost hung up while waiting for him to come on the line. She inhaled a deep breath and forced herself to wait for him.

"Dakota, what can I do for you?" His bass voice jolted her, it sounded much deeper over the phone.

"Thank you for taking my call. I know…I…it's…I mean…" She gathered her courage. "Is that invitation to the concert still open?"

"Yes, of course."

"I'd like to go." The line went quiet for several moments.

"Wonderful. I'd like nothing better." He sounded happy. "Do you want to know who we're going to see?"

"No. I just need to get out and have a good time."

"Didn't you enjoy last weekend?"

"Yes, of course I did. But I need to get out, in the world." She stopped. "Wait, that didn't sound the way I meant. I mean I want to go out with you and I'd be happy to see anyone."

"It's a jazz concert at the Keswick. Several artists." If he talked to her all night, she didn't care who they went to see. She'd just listen to the musical sound of his voice.

"I'll pick you up on Saturday at seven."

"I'll be ready. Oh, and Bishop, can I get your number? I don't want to have to call the assistant if I need to talk with you."

"Then you intend to call me again? I hope you won't call to cancel."

She chuckled. He made her laugh at the silliest things. "I won't cancel."

After he gave her his phone number, she hung up feeling like she had just taken a ride on a roller coaster.

§§§

Bishop placed the phone on the receiver and listened to the sound his beard made as he rubbed his hand across his chin. He hadn't expected that call. She seemed so emphatic with her refusal. Maybe that's what drew him to Dakota — her unpredictability. The way she laughed at the simplest things or the way she tilted her head when she was giving something serious thought. She was refreshing, different from all the cookie-cutter women he'd dated. Instead of all the primping, preening, and eyeing of his wallet, she didn't seem the least bit interested in his status or his bank account. She was happier with her VW Beetle, hummus and chips, instead of luxury cars and prime rib. A sense of satisfaction washed over him.

Simeon tapped on the half-open door and stepped into his office. Without waiting to be asked, he took the seat next to the desk and planted his foot on his knee.

"I didn't get a chance to formally thank you for taking my sister-in-law home." Simeon said.

"No problem. Glad I could help."

"Dakota mentioned you might help her with the renovations at her store. I like that idea." He nodded with approval.

100

"I'm working on some ideas." Bishop reached for his tablet.

"You've been to the store already?" Simeon sounded surprised.

"This morning. She wants to get started right away. That's not a problem, is it?"

He waited a moment before replying. "I…I don't guess so. But she's going through some things right now and I just hope she's not being impulsive. Take it slow. She might change her mind in a few weeks and want something totally different." Simeon stood and leaned against the file cabinet. "How's everything else going? Have you had a chance to talk with Asa about the fashion show set? The date is approaching fast."

"I'll contact her today."

After they discussed his other projects, Simeon exited his office. Bishop twirled his pen through his fingers as he contemplated Simeon's words. Was their conversation strictly regarding Dakota's bookstore or was Simeon also talking about her personal life?

Bishop dropped the pen on the desk. No matter what, he'd take it slow, handle her with special care, until he was sure she was ready. If she only wanted a fling, he was willing to play along, but the thought made his stomach constrict.

His phone rang. He yanked the receiver up hoping Dakota was calling again.

"Bishop, how's it going?" His sister's cheerful voice came across the line.

"Adanna, what's up?"

"I know you're real busy, but Dennis is running late tonight and I need to go to the store. We're out of formula. Can you take me before you head to Philly, can you take me?"

"Sure, no problem. If you give me your list, I can just pick up stuff for you." He poised his pen, ready to jot down her items.

"You know how I like to wander the aisles. Besides, you never get the brands I want. And you don't know how to pick out fruit. I'd rather do it myself. Also, I have a woman I want to talk to you about. I met her at DJ's play group."

He laughed at his sister. "Adanna, I still think you and Dennis need to buy a car. At least give the idea some thought."

"Yeah, but will you, do take me? I need formula, not a lecture, big brother."

"I'll see you this evening. By the way, I never agreed to your matchmaking service. I can handle my love life without any help. No offense."

"I'm not offended. But you know I'm just as bullheaded as you are, so stop complaining."

Instead of responding, Bishop ended the conversation. His sister sounded a lot tougher than she was. The only time she asserted herself was when something pertained to him. She needed to use some of that authority on her husband.

Somehow, Adanna had missed all Dad's words of wisdom. While she was busy playing with her dolls, their father had ushered him and his brothers onto the corner basketball court for a mini life lesson. According to him, all you needed in life was women and wealth, but not necessarily in that order. When his mother was steaming mad at their father, she preached respect and caring. These two lessons had him equipped for life.

With his tablet opened on his desk, he found the contact list and dialed Asa's number. After a brief conversation where she did all the talking, he shut down his office and headed out.

Bishop pulled up to her townhouse and as expected, Adanna wasn't waiting. He dialed her number.

"I'm putting my coat on now. I'll be right out." She hung up without saying goodbye. With the diaper bag in one arm and the baby nestled into the car seat on her other arm, she lumbered down the stairs.

Once she buckled the baby into the backseat, she climbed in and pulled the door closed so hard he jumped. "What is that all about and why are you taking it out on my car?"

She folded her arms over her chest. Unshed tears filled her eyes and she bit her bottom lip to keep from crying.

"Mom."

"What happened now?" He put the car in park and waited.

"I literally begged her to come for a visit during the holidays. She flat-out refuses. I can't believe her," she croaked.

"I asked you to give her some time, Adanna. She won't stay mad at you forever. I'll give her a call in a few weeks. Maybe I can convince her."

"I told her that Dennis and I would come see her and she pooh-poohed that idea too. If you ask her, I bet she'd jump on a plane and be here within a day."

"Calm down before you get DJ upset. I'll talk to her." He rubbed his sister's arm, hoping to placate her.

She wrapped her arms around her waist. Her breathing was loud and labored. Adanna held on to emotions like a baby with a bottle.

"I called you all weekend. So what bimbo were you with this time? Jill? Becka?"

"That's none of your business. And she was not a bimbo." He put the car in drive. As long as she was railing against him, at least she wasn't crying over their mother.

"I think your behavior is disgusting." She huffed.

She didn't have any objections."

"I guess not. What did you buy her?"

"Chinese food."

She glared at him. "Dad was lucky Mom stuck around while he acted like a fool. Don't think you'll find a good woman willing to put up with that kind of nonsense."

"Thanks for your unsolicited advice." He chuckled at his sister's insistence. They remained silent for the rest of the drive.

Together they walked into the store. "You go ahead and shop. I'll hold my nephew." He lifted the sleeping baby from his sister's arms. DJ rested his head on Bishop's chest.

He strolled behind his sister as she threw items in the shopping cart.

"Are you mad at me or Mom? And who's paying for all that stuff?" He nodded to the half-full cart.

"I'm mad at Mom. I'm always mad at her. And you're paying. Dennis doesn't get paid until Friday. Can you help me out?" Her large brown eyes cut right to her heart.

"What makes you any different from the other women that keep trying to get in my wallet?"

"I'm your sister." She shoved his arm and the tears she tried to hold back spilled down her face. He draped his free arm around her shoulder.

"Everything is going to be okay, sis. Please don't get too upset. You know how Mom can be. I promise she'll see DJ soon, even if I have to charter a plane and fly us all out to La Jolla, California." He tightened his arms around her. He hated when women cried. Especially women he loved.

Chapter Ten

Dakota parked her car and jumped out. She ran to the door of the Whole Foods Market while pulling her coat around her neck. She only needed a few items to replace everything she and Bishop had munched over the weekend to keep their strength up.

In the dairy, she looked for the expiration date on the bottom of the container of hummus. Without finding the information she threw the plastic container into the basket swinging from her arm and headed to the coffee aisle. Every trip to the store encouraged her to buy something more.

Her buoyant disposition felt good after a year of living a cloistered life. In one wild ride over a reckless weekend, she'd blown away the cobwebs collecting on her life. Next she'd call Sunny and Tora to see what her girlfriends were up to.

Getting Brian's tape back from Simeon needled her. But what would she do with the darn thing? Play the message from time to time and think about the mistake she'd almost made? Or would she take it to some teenage group home and tell the girls to stay away from men who could break their hearts? The signs were always there. One shouldn't have ignored them.

Maybe next week she'd call Simeon and ask for the tape after all. Nobody would ever believe that something so dramatic could happen to her, so she might need the tape as proof.

Dakota rounded the corner, heading to the registers, resisting the urge to whistle. From the corner of her eye, she spotted someone who should have been familiar, but something was off. At the end of the aisle, she watched Bishop rub the back of a sleeping baby while hugging an attractive young woman with long straight hair. She watched as the woman closed in on Bishop and kissed the sleeping baby.

Her heart thumped against her ribs at almost the same time her knees decided not to work. The sound of rushing water flooded her ears and for what seemed like minutes, but was only moments she couldn't draw a single thought that made sense. The urge to walk over to him and slap his bearded face surged through her veins. Why had he asked her out if he was seeing someone? She struggled for a breath and spun away from the touching scene in the middle of the store.

"Damn it, Dakota," she uttered as shame claimed her.

At least she hadn't fallen in love. She'd only stuck her toe in the pool of Bishop. Just like all the other women before her. It felt good for the half second it lasted. But he'd only screwed her good and proper then invited her to a concert, not to be the love of his life. She shook her head, pushing away the icy reality that swept over her.

To think she would move from one disastrous relationship to the perfect union was ridiculous. Being out of the dating market for a while, she'd forgotten how cruel men could be. Memories of her girlfriends crying and distraught about dating deceptions came rushing back.

She sucked her tongue as she dropped her basket at her feet. Getting out of the store before Bishop saw her was the only thing that mattered.

"Sir." She signaled a clerk walking by. "I think I'm going to be sick, can you please put these items back on the shelf for me?" Without waiting for a reply, she darted to the nearest exit.

In the car, she put all the windows down and gulped crisp fresh air. This was silly. She shouldn't be upset. But he hadn't told the truth. If he could lie so easily for a romp with a woman he'd just met, what was he willing to do when there was more at stake? She never envisioned him as untrustworthy, but the touching scene in the market told her everything she needed to know.

She backed out of the space without checking her rearview mirror. The chances that she'd get dumped and run into Mr. Perfect were higher than her chances of winning the lottery. She might as well slow down and enjoy what came her way without thinking every hello or concert invitation was a love connection.

In front of her house, Dakota turned off the car and ran up the stairs. Her appetite had faded. She marched up to the bedroom and fell backwards on the bed. With her arms folded behind her head, she kicked off her shoes.

"What were you thinking, silly goose?" she said. "Of course he has a girlfriend. Maybe several." She slapped her leg. Being out of commission had dulled her dating senses. The next time around, she vowed to be more astute before accepting a date. No matter how good looking or smooth talking he appeared on the outside, she'd ask the standard twenty questions. Starting with, are you married? Are you dating? Are you a father?

The phone rang. She hesitated for moment before picking up the receiver.

"Dakota, I'll be in Delaware in a few weeks. I hope to be there for the opening of the community center." Melissa never said hello. She assumed everyone knew her voice and was glad to hear from her.

"Great." Dakota continued to stare at the ceiling.

"What's wrong with you? Don't you want me to come?" Melissa's tone was sharp.

"Of course I do. I haven't seen you since Fashion Week. I'm just bummed about my love life falling apart and sounding chipper is hard"

"What happened?"

She relayed the Brian story and the Whole Foods story to her sister without shedding a tear.

"I'm sorry, Dakota." Melissa's sincerity was more than Dakota expected.

"Don't be. I'm fine. The timing stinks. Brian and I were history months ago, we just made it official. And I just accepted a date with Bishop today. I don't love him or anything, but I should have followed my instincts when I originally said no." She took a breath. "Anyway, I'll cancel tomorrow. No harm, no foul."

"If it makes you feel any better, Darius is being a royal jerk. That's another reason why I've decided to get out of town for a while. Maybe if I give him a chance to miss me, he'll appreciate me more."

"Come as soon as you can, we can sit around together and trade war stories. I bet mine will top yours any day."

§§§

Donuts would have been a nice touch for such a gloomy day, but the last thing Dakota needed was to feel cheery. There was some comfort in wallowing in the doldrums. At least this way she had no expectations and nothing was a surprise. She would scrounge up the courage to cancel the date with Bishop. Maybe she'd even include a recommendation that he take the stunning beauty he was hugging in the grocery store to the concert.

She unlocked the doors of the bookstore and flipped on the lights. In her office, she secured her knapsack to the back of the chair before pulling open the desk drawers. She found the cheesecloth filled with sage. After checking that the end was secure with twine she lit the bundle.

The earthy smell penetrated her nostrils as she waved the rags throughout out the space. With all the disappointment she'd experienced, she wanted

113

to cleanse the bookstore, chase away the bad spirits, and invite happier ones in.

Through the large plate glass window, she saw Bishop approach the door. As usual, his swagger was confident and today he wore a custom-fit gray suit that matched the color of the fall sky. With his tablet tucked under his arm, he popped open the front door.

Too bad he was taken, because even now he made her mouth water. But neglecting to tell her he was in a relationship spoke to his character. Why he chose to conceal his relationship chomped at her sense of fair play. How could he be a playboy? If his relationships were built on lies and deception, he wouldn't make it very far. She shrugged, better to know now, before wasting any time.

He saw Dakota and waved. "Sure smells good in here. Like…" He sniffed. "Like…"

"This is sage," Dakota said without looking up. She refused to gush. As far as she was concerned, he was just another good-looking man. She'd have many of them cross her path, no need to get wobbly kneed every time.

"I like the scent. But what does it do?" He stood on the opposite side of the counter.

"The aura in the bookstore is in a bad place. I'm chasing away the bad karma. I did my house this morning. Now, I'm doing the bookstore." She continued to wave the rag.

"Do you think this works?" He scratched his chin.

"Time will tell." She blew on the tip of the rag to extinguish the flame.

He opened his tablet. "I'm not too early, am I?"

"Not at all. Let me see what you've got." She propped her elbows on the counter and placed her chin in her palm. "Stick to business," she mumbled so he wouldn't hear.

"Do you want to come around to this side? You'll be able to see better."

"No, this is fine." The more distance between them the better.

He scrolled through several designs explaining each one in great detail. Dakota was only half listening. She wanted to scream at him for lying to her. Instead she nodded throughout his presentation and pretended everything was normal.

"I like this one the best." She pointed to the second design with several small reading sections and lots of pot ceiling lights. The dark wood floor added warmth to the space.

"That's the one I would have chosen too." He gave her one of his electrifying smiles.

She sat back and eyed him. Maybe that wasn't the best one for her. Obviously he didn't have good judgment. "Then maybe I need to take a little more time and think about all three designs." There was an edge in her voice that she hadn't expected.

"Is something wrong, Dakota? You seem distracted today. If this is not a good time we can do this another day."

She shifted her position to get a better look at his face. He seemed to be very calm. Either he was a professional prevaricator or he didn't care.

Confronting him was not her style. Melissa used to tease her, calling her a wuss because she'd come home crying instead of facing down a problem.

She squared her shoulders. "Look, I can't do this."

"You don't like any of these designs?"

"No. I can't work with you. I'll have a talk with Simeon about finding someone else for me to work with." She shoved his tablet towards him.

"The designs can't be that bad," He scratched his chin. "Let me know what you don't like and I'll work up something new."

"Look, I know we aren't a couple or anything." She tried to swallow the knot in her throat. "So you had no reason to lie to me. After this weekend I had no expectations other than the truth. I know you're a womanizer, but I thought you only had one woman at a time. That, I could deal with. But your life is a circus."

He looked over his shoulder at the door. "Circus? What are you talking about?"

She released a dismissive sigh. "I saw you last night in Whole Foods."

"Ah, you should have come over to me. I could have introduced you to my sister. She's only been in town a few months and doesn't know many people."

"Your sister?" Her cheeks grew warm.

His eyes widened. "You thought that was a girlfriend, didn't you?" His laughter filled the store.

"It's not that funny."

"Yes it is." He continued to laugh, holding his hand to his mouth. "You're funny. You should see yourself. You're pouting like a kid who doesn't want to take a nap. What did you think—I asked you out, then went home to my other woman? I'm not trying to hurt anyone or get hurt. I told you that."

"I've been told a lot of things." She crossed her arms to channel her indignation.

"Not by me." His smiled disappeared, replaced by a more serious expression. "So that's what this is all about." He pointed to the distance between them. "You haven't gotten near me all morning."

"How was I supposed to know?"

"You're supposed to trust me."

She swallowed while trying to keep the emotion from showing in her face. When did she become that woman who suspected the worst in everything and everyone? "I trusted before and look what happened."

"I don't know what happened in your last relationship, but I'm not your ex."

She nodded her concession. "You're right. I'm sorry."

"Did you just apologize? I don't think I've ever heard a woman do that before."

"Well, I'm different, too. I do a lot of things other women don't."

"Well, I don't do a lot of things other men do." His voice was softer as he mocked her. He walked around the counter. For a moment, he looked down at her before kissing her forehead, then her mouth with the same blistering desire that blazed in his eyes.

After a minute, he released her. She ran her tongue over her lips. His proclamation captured her heart. She grabbed the wooden counter to keep from swooning. Everything was moving so fast. She had little time to sort it out.

"The baby is your nephew?"

He nodded. "DJ."

"DJ? What does that stand for?"

"Dennis Jr. He's named after his father. I'd like to introduce you to Adanna and her family."

When had her instincts become so bad? She used to pride herself on the ability to read people or see bad news coming long before it arrived. At least she hadn't made a complete fool of herself by approaching him in the store. She hoped Bishop didn't think she was one of those women spewing accusations with little knowledge.

"Sure, I'd love to meet your sister." She tried to sound normal, as if she had fully recovered from the whole episode. "Let me think about the designs. I should know which one I want in a few days."

"I understand. There's no rush." He gave her an odd look as if she might be one of those fickle women who never knew what they wanted.

"I'm sure I can make a decision. How hard can choosing be? I just need a little time to digest this information."

"What information? The bookstore, or me?" He crossed his ankles and leaned against the counter.

"Both." She barely heard her own voice.

"Come here." He pulled her into his arms. "I won't hurt you. It's not possible."

Chapter Eleven

Bishop pushed away from the computer. The week had dragged out like a long boring movie, but tonight was the night. The last time he was this excited about a date was back when he was still in college. Something interesting was happening between him and Dakota. It felt right and wrong all at once, like playing golf in the rain with his church clothes on. His goal was to remain unattached and uninvolved, but every time Dakota came within inches of him, she made his declaration harder to keep.

He glanced at his watch. If he didn't leave soon, he would be late picking up Dakota for the concert. He checked his pocket, making sure the concert tickets were in place.

Simeon's words echoed in his head about her needing time and going slow. If that's what she needed, he was willing to do whatever was necessary. Dakota didn't seem to notice her understated charm and seduction. That's what made her so attractive. All the smooth moves that worked so easily on other women weren't effective on her. He grabbed his car keys and headed out the door. She only lived a few blocks from Harper

Enterprise. He'd never even noticed the bookstore before he met her. How he could have missed Dakota still boggled him.

She stood on the top step in front of her townhouse. Her jacket collar was pulled up against a tomato-red scarf. The matching mittens made her look younger. As soon as he pulled up, she charged down the stairs and hopped into the passenger seat. Her hair was curled tighter than normal and her luscious lips were a muted shade of red."

"You could be Little Red Riding Hood's sister." He laughed.

"I'm trying to stay warm."

"It's not that cold. Why were you waiting outside? I'd planned to come to the door and knock like a proper gentleman," he said.

"Oh, I was excited about tonight and was dressed, so I…I." she stuttered.

He continued. "I don't think I've ever heard another woman admit being excited about a date with me. I thought that wasn't cool. I've been looking forward to tonight, too." He shifted into gear and pulled away from the curb.

With a shoulder shrug, her lips curved into an innocent smile. "I have some old-fashioned ways.

Just so you know, when I bring you home, I'll be walking you to the door."

"A proper gentleman. I don't know if I've seen one of them in eons. At least now I know what one looks like. You know you're almost extinct?" She gave him a radiant smile.

"There are probably more of us around than you know. We like to keep a low profile."

Her bubbly personality was back. The light hint of joy in her voice promised a fun night. It was the only thing he could think about all day. Even the work on Asa's design for the fashion show seemed secondary. The urge to wrap his arms around her intensified.

"I'll remember that. So tell me who are we going to see tonight? I know you started to tell me before, but I was still in a haze."

"So you're using me for fun?"

"Can I be honest?" she asked. Without waiting for him to reply, she continued. "You've been a pleasant distraction. I can't remember the last time I had fun with someone of the opposite sex, I would have gone with you to see a kiddie movie."

"What about last Saturday and Sunday?" He hoped her response came close to what she was feeling.

"Let me see," she paused. "How can I categorize my behavior? You saved an extremely horny woman from another night of loneliness. I think I'll leave the rest to your imagination"

"Not the answer I was hoping for." His stomach tightened.

"What should I have said?"

"I don't know. You're the one who reads the romance letters. You could have come up with something more compelling."

"Let me see. My heart quivered at the sight of you. My body longs for your touch." She giggled.

"Okay smarty pants. I get it. Quiver? Nobody uses that word anymore." He glanced at her. "Glad I could be there for you. It's what we real gentlemen like doing best." He made the left turn on Keswick Avenue. His sister seemed to think only men had commitment issues. Dakota was in that class of people too. Good company and a romp in the sheets might be the only thing she needed. Maybe he'd met his match. He could fall for her. Easily.

"Tonight we're going to see a medley of jazz artists. I hope you like jazz."

"I'm not into music too much. As you can see, I'm a book person, but I'm looking forward to the concert."

"I'll tell you all about the music, and later, I'll let you share your world of books with me."

"Deal." She held up her fist for him to tap.

He found a parking lot a block away from the theater. With his hand on her back, they weaved through the crowd mingling outside, smoking their last cigarettes before heading in.

The atmosphere inside the lobby grew more festive. People milled around before making their way to their seats.

"I don't think I've been to a concert since I was in college. Even then, I couldn't tell you the name of the group I saw. We were just a bunch of girls on a wild night out." Dakota took the interior seat.

"I feel honored then."

The lights dimmed and the concert emcee took the stage to introduce the first act. The music was too loud to have a conversation but Dakota swayed with the beat and each time bumped his arm in rhythm with the music. She looked at him and mouthed something he couldn't understand. He pointed to his ear and shook his head. Instead of repeating her gesture she leaned across the seat and kissed him. Her sweet tongue lingered against his. The lights came up midway through the show for intermission.

They were slow to stand. "You look like you're enjoying yourself," he said.

She continued to shake her hips even though the only music was canned. "I am. This is fantastic. I can't believe I've been missing so much."

"Let's walk to the lobby. You look like you could use some popcorn."

"You're right. I could." She slipped out of the seat and into the aisle.

They fell in line behind the procession to the front of the theater. He reached back for her small hand.

"Gosh, I didn't realize I was hungry until I smelled the popcorn," she said as they stood at the end of the concession line.

From the far side of the lobby, he spotted Sharon. Heat crept up his spine and settled on his neck. Their eyes locked for a moment too long. He stiffened as she headed his way. If she intended to create a scene, he wasn't up for her nonsense tonight. If his father taught him little else, he drilled in the idea of discretion. It was now part of his mantra, just like the Boy Scout oath and his pledge to stay unattached. If he couldn't keep his business private, he might as well get married, then there was nothing to keep to himself. Words of wisdom from his father.

"Hey, Bishop." Her familiar sing-song voice rang out his name.

"Hello, Sharon."

Dakota stepped away from him. Her eyes widened. He tightened his hold on her hand, pulling her closer.

"Sharon, I'd like you to meet a good friend of mine, Dakota Conroy."

Dakota stuck out her hand with a big smile. "Hi, Sharon."

Sharon shook her hand without looking at Dakota.

Bishop inched forward in line, hoping Sharon would move on. Instead she planted her stiletto heeled feet just inches from his foot.

"So, how have you been, Bishop? I've been trying to get in touch with you. Did your sister give you my messages?" Sharon rested her hand on his arm.

Without removing her hand, he focused his attention on her. "Sharon, as you can see, I'm pretty busy right now. How's everything between you and Richard?"

"Richard's history."

"Sorry to hear that. Take care of yourself." He shifted his body until her hand fell. He wrapped his arm around Dakota's waist and stepped to the popcorn counter. Several seconds ticked by before Sharon rolled her eyes and strutted away. "A friend of yours, huh?" Dakota asked.

"An old friend."

"Old as in dear?" Dakota positioned her body to stare at him.

"No, old as in a long time ago." A prickle of perspiration peppered his neck. He stuck his finger inside his collar, loosening the material. The look she gave him said she didn't believe his story. "Do you think you will ever be able to trust me?" He paid for the popcorn and soda.

"You've done nothing inappropriate." She placed a piece of popcorn in her mouth. "I'm not as delicate as I look."

"Good to know."

"But don't push me, Bishop." She chuckled and plucked another piece of popcorn from the bag.

"Have I given you any reason not to trust me?" He maneuvered her back into the theater as the lights blinked, signaling the start of the show. "What happened to innocent until proven guilty?"

"Life." She took her seat. "But you saw the look on Sharon's face. She hasn't let you go, yet."

Her eyes revealed fear. It was the look he'd seen in his sister's eyes when she'd told him she was pregnant. The only difference was Dakota didn't try to hide her emotions.

"Sharon broke off our relationship when she started dating a player on the Nets basketball team. My guess is that relationship is over, and she's surfing for someone else to warm her bed."

"Wow, that's harsh."

"That's the truth."

The emcee announced the next act as the lights went down.

As soon as the music started, Dakota was out of her seat, swinging her hips with the thump, thump, thump of the drums. Her infectious enthusiasm made it easy to forget Sharon's annoying interruption. Each time Dakota shook her hips, they telegraphed a message to his groin. When they were together, his brain shifted into calculating mode, thinking of ways to extend their time together. He wouldn't admit it to anyone, but they weren't just hanging out, having a good time. She was under his skin and he enjoyed the rush. By the time the lights came on at the end of the show, the two of them had laughed and hummed along with each of the artists.

"Are you hungry?" He held her close as they made their way back to the car.

"I'm starved. I didn't have time to eat before you picked me up."

"Then maybe I ought to feed you." He planted an innocent kiss on her temple. Dakota Conroy was something special. She could throw him off his game.

§§§

Dakota liked the way Bishop guided her to the car with his hand positioned on her lower back. The pressure he applied sent ripples up her spine, with a tremendous sense that they were a couple. She backed that thought out of her head. No matter how special he made her feel, she couldn't assume this wasn't just part of his style, part of his cache to attract women. He knew how to make women feel special, all playboys did.

She glanced up. His solid chin was slightly lifted against the cold. He stuck his hand in her coat pocket.

"I'm trying to stay warm." He grinned and flashed his even white teeth.

"See, you thought I was crazy with the scarf and the mittens, didn't you?"

"Really, this is just an excuse to get closer to you." He tightened his hand on her waist.

"You don't need an excuse." She unwound her scarf and wrapped the two of them in it.

They were more of a couple than she and Brian had ever been. With Brian, she always had the sense he'd held a small piece of himself back. Bishop's in-your-face desire was refreshing. Even if their relationship didn't lead to forever, she wanted to enjoy every moment while they lasted.

When they approached the car she realized, as always, she was moving fast. Thinking about a future with him was lethal. She closed her eyes for a second, trying to focus on the present. She couldn't stop her active imagination from pulling up images of Bishop every hour of every day.

She still heard the music pounding in her ears even though the concert had ended an hour ago. "I may have an earache tomorrow."

"That's the downside of a concert." He pulled the car out of the lot. "Other than a little deafness, you shouldn't have any other side effects."

"Deafness? You make that sound like no big thing."

"Look at it this way, if everyone in our generation is going to concerts, we'll all be deaf. So we can just talk louder. We can always stand around and compare who has the latest and greatest in hearing aid technology."

His nonchalant attitude toward something so serious lightened her heart. He didn't feel the need to let life weigh him down. The hearty sound of her own laughter made her laugh even more. He joined her. Without taking his eyes off the traffic, his chuckle started out slow, but within seconds, the two of them could barely catch their breath.

"I can't remember the last time I had such so much fun," she managed between gasps.

"What about—"

"In public. I'm talking about in public." She swatted his arm.

"Oh. That's better. Because I was laying my smoothest moves on you the other night."

"So, you're not always such an attentive lover?"

"I didn't say that. Pleasing you was the only thing I could think about last weekend."

She pressed the palm of her hand against her chest. "Are you serious? You're just trying to talk your way back into my panties aren't you?"

Bishop looked at her without expression. The car behind them honked when the light changed and he didn't accelerate.

"You don't have much regard for me, do you?"

"That's not true. I haven't spent much time around such a ladies' man, so all my knowledge comes from movies I've seen."

"Well believe it or not, most of that stuff isn't true. At least not as far as I'm concerned."

"You take such a carefree approach to everything," She was serious now, too.

"Why not? I never want to take myself too serious. That night at Simeon's house, you said you were going to be different. I was trying to be helpful."

Dakota stared at him. With her hands folded in her lap, she drew a deep breath. He was right. So far, she'd kept her vow. But the more time they spent together, the more she wanted him.

This was fun. Her old self was returning. Their future was limited. She'd have to time their exit just right before she got hurt.

Her sisters thought she was a scatterbrain. She didn't mind the nickname. Their endless list of things they needed to accomplish weighed them down. Unlike them, she took life as it presented itself. Conquering problems that hadn't materialized was pointless. Tonight, Bishop only seemed interested in making sure she had a good time. The attention was well worth the thumping in her ears. She wrapped her arms around her waist. She was playing with fire, but couldn't back away from his hypnotizing charm.

The vision of Sharon nagged at her. The way she laid her hand on his arm and the intense look in her eyes declared ownership. If they weren't still seeing each other, it wasn't because she didn't want to.

"What would you like to eat?" He drew her out of her thoughts.

"Let's see." She pretended to give her choice great consideration. "How about pizza? We can stop at Tony's. I think they're still open." She leaned over to glance at the clock on the dashboard.

"Okay. Now that I've shared my music with you, you have to tell me, what is your favorite book of all time?" When he smiled, his whole face changed. His eyes sparkled.

"Oh, now that's a tough one. My customers ask me that all the time and I'm always reluctant to tell them. I don't want to influence their opinions."

"I'm really curious. Can a bookstore owner have a favorite?"

"I guess I'd have to say my favorite is Gloria Naylor. She wrote *Mama Day*." Dakota looked at him to see his response. "Have you heard of her? I honestly could not put that book down."

"No. But most of my reading is on designs and architecture, so I can't be a judge." He pulled into the parking lot of Tony's. With the late hour, the place was nearly deserted. He turned off the car and focused his attention on her. "Why is that your favorite?"

"You really want to know?"

"I do."

"When I first read the book, the story scared the hell out of me. My family used to talk about people working voodoo on each other. I always thought it was just a big joke. But that book made me wonder…"

"So that's what's going on here. You must have put some kind of spell on me that night at your place. I can't seem to get enough of you." He stroked the top of her hand.

She snatched her hand away and swatted him. "You wish. I think you took a lock of my hair and put it in your shoe, just so I'd follow you."

"It's working, huh?" He laughed as he opened his door and walked around to open hers. "Are you superstitious?" They walked to the front door of the small Italian restaurant.

"Well, I don't walk under ladders or cross black cats, if that's what you mean. And from now on, I'm making sure I know where every strand of my hair is at all times."

"Not to worry. As long as you're following me, I'll take good care of you." They took a seat at a table jammed in the corner of the small restaurant. Instead of sitting in the chair across from her, he squeezed into the one beside her.

They sat so close, his arm brushed her shoulder. She removed her leather jacket to feel his heat. She couldn't get enough of him. Talking to a man in person was much better than the long distance relationship she'd had with Brian. She felt like a castaway making human contact for the first time in months.

"What do you want on your pie?" His breath smelled liked popcorn. She searched his luscious lips. The intensity in his brown eyes was close to hypnotic. She would have been content with eating cardboard.

"It's after midnight. I can't eat meat this late."

He cocked his head to one side. "Why not?"

"Just can't. I won't sleep a wink if I do."

"Then let's order the extra meat pizza. I don't think we're getting much sleep tonight anyway."

He lifted her chin with the tip of his index finger and his lips captured her mouth. Their tongues engaged in a friendly battle, just like their banter. She shifted in her seat to squash the desire blooming between her legs.

Chapter Twelve

The empty pizza tin and soiled napkins cluttered the table. Bishop looked happy. The evening had been great and he didn't need to spend a gob of money to make her smile. The server removed the empty pizza tray from the table. Bishop had agreed to eat a vegetable pizza to please her, even though she knew he would have preferred some beef and pork. Just that simple gesture made her drape her arms around his neck and kiss him.

"So, are you spending the night with me?" Bishop wrapped his arm around her shoulder.

"I can't. I don't even have a toothbrush." She didn't sound convincing, but she needed to slow down. They were moving too fast. "I can get you anything you need."

"What, do you keep extra panties at your house in all sizes just in case?" She placed her napkin on the table.

"You'll only need a toothbrush. Believe me, you won't need panties."

She contemplated his comment with a twist of her lips. She wouldn't say no. Even if she could form the word, she couldn't vocalize the sentiment.

"Do you have hummus?" She moved her face close to his.

"I will by the time you want some." He pushed away from the table and helped her put on her coat. After wrapping the bright red scarf around her neck they walked out into the cold night air to the car. She held him tight for his warmth and because she couldn't deny her budding attraction to him.

During the ride from the restaurant, she chatted like a nervous teenager while wringing her hands. He held her still by grabbing her arm. "Why are you so fidgety?"

"I was thinking about the incident at the concert with your ex-girlfriend. Does that kind of thing happen a lot with you?"

"No. And it shouldn't matter. How many times will I need to tell you that?"

She placed her hands at her sides. "Until I get it."

How long will that take?"

"Are you getting tired already? She stuck her neck out, but her tone was playful.

"I'll say it ten more times. After that, I'm done." He pulled into the garage at his house and put the car in park.

She shook her head in agreement, but her eyes revealed she was far from believing him.

The serious expression on her face let him know she was still processing his comment. Childlike innocence sparkled in her eyes and touched his heart. He wasn't supposed to feel this way. Years of observing relationships had taught him they were fraught with complication. Something he wanted no part of. Hassle-free was the way he lived his life

At the condo, he held the door open. She made full-body contact as she brushed by him with a laugh.

"What's funny?" He walked behind her, turning on the lights along the way.

"I can't believe we're doing this."

"Doing what?"

"Spending the night together again. Will this be another marathon weekend?" She unbuttoned her coat.

He pushed her coat off her shoulders and hung it in the entry closet along with his. "If that's what you want." He pinned her against the wall and lifted her chin. Her luscious mouth invited him to run his tongue over her full lips before slipping in. Every kiss felt like the first one. He caressed her right breast through her thick sweater and listened as she purred like a pleased kitten.

He tugged her sweater free of her jeans to slip his hand underneath. Touching her warm flesh stirred his desire. His erection pressed against his pants, straining the fabric. He released her breast and pulled her top up without releasing her mouth. He wanted to take his time and enjoy every minute with her. She wasn't a beauty for the night just to warm his bed and then bid goodbye.

"What's the matter?" she asked.

He shook his head, not ready to find words to explain what was going on in his head. "How about a glass of wine?"

In the kitchen, he turned on the light, flooding the room with a bright glow.

"No. I don't want wine. I had what I want back there in the entryway." She positioned herself on the barstool and adjusted her sweater back in place.

"Let me get a glass of water." He recognized what was happening. He sucked the air out of his stomach to push the overwhelming desire away. Lust was easier to deal with than love. Lust he understood, love was different. Love made you weak, his mother and sister were proof. Losing control wasn't supposed to happen to him. Not now. Not with Dakota. Not ever.

He filled the glass from the faucet and took a swallow and then pushed the glass across the quartz counter to her.

Before taking a drink she stared at him, her large brown eyes filled with questions. This wasn't the first time a woman tried to pin him down, the oppressive stench of commitment was in the air, hovering over him like a buzzard.

"Read me one of those letters. I'd like to hear one."

"You're kidding me, right? Now?"

"I'm serious. I shared my passion for music with you, now I want to know what you find so interesting about letters someone else has written."

She reached on the back of her chair for her knapsack and pulled out a thin, well-worn paperback book.

"From the size of that book, there aren't many letters."

"This is just one volume. There are hundreds of them and if you keep getting smart with me, I'll read them all to you." She grinned.

"Okay, I'm teasing. Go ahead." If letting her read the letter would take his mind off of their relationship, he could listen.

"Here's a letter that Ludwig van Beethoven wrote in the 1800s, but no one knows who he wrote to, '*My angel, my all, my very self— only a few words today and at that with your pencil—not 'til tomorrow will my lodgings be definitely determined upon—what a useless waste of time. Why this deep sorrow where necessity speaks—can our love endure except through sacrifices—except through not demanding everything— can you change it that you are not wholly mine, I not wholly thine?*' Doesn't that sound intriguing? Just listen to the way he started the letter."

He nodded. "That's pretty awesome. I'll stick with non-fiction, but I can see why women might like that kind of thing."

"Oh, you think love is just a woman thing?"

"You won't find many men that like that kind of thing, now will you?"

With one hand she fanned the pages of the book. "All these letters were written by men. I have several more volumes at home. So the answer to your question would be, yes. If a man knows what he wants, then he might like this kind of thing." She reached for the glass of water and drained the contents. She stood, scraping the stool legs against the floor.

He massaged between his brows with his thumb. Being a jerk to deflect the commitment conversation was despicable, but to treat Dakota this way was even more disgusting. She was always so open with her feelings, so he needed to step up his game. At times like this, it was easier to blame his parents for his aversion to relationships. Hiding behind his father's infidelity was a thin sham. It was getting harder and harder to place his burden on his father's shoulders.

Whenever a woman got close, he backed away. But the last thing he wanted to do was hurt Dakota.

"Nice place you have here." She strolled over to the floor-to-ceiling windows while admiring his oil paintings. "Why am I not surprised that you have nude paintings on your living room wall?" She spun around. Her eyes were dark and unreadable.

"You're joking, right? Those pictures are gorgeous. This is fine art." He waved at the canvases, glad the awkward moment had passed. She could have been the model in any one of the portraits on the wall. The soft curves of her butt and breasts made her perfect hourglass figure worthy of immortalizing

"And I suppose you have Playboy magazines stuffed under your mattress and you read them for the articles."

A picture of her as a centerfold flashed across his mind, drawing an instant response from his gut. He grabbed her around the waist. "Let's go see." He picked her up and carried her down the hall towards the bedroom. The sound of her giggles as he walked to the end of hall was the only noise in the condo.

On the bed, she sat up to unbuckle his belt. "You're getting undressed first this time." She unzipped his pants and pushed them down his legs.

"No problem. I like a woman who knows what she wants." He removed his remaining clothes one piece at a time until he stood before her naked. The way her eyes covered his body was both sexy and naughty. Her tongue darted over her lips, beckoning him forward.

"Perfect." She didn't hide the lust in her eyes as she looked him over.

He reached for her turtleneck and pulled it over her head. "Now it's your turn." After unhooking her bra, he cupped her full breasts, one in each hand. He kissed one nipple and her skin pebbled under his lips. He switched to the other breast with the same results.

Using the pads of her fingers, she kneaded his back, releasing the tension along his spine. The warmth from the closeness of her body mingled with his as he pulled her into his arms. A slow burn of desire started in the pit of his stomach. Blood rushed to his loins, waking every nerve. His engorged member sprung to life against her thigh. With his mouth partly open, he covered her lips. The only thing he could focus on was taking her in, her smell, her taste, her feel.

His raw emotions surfaced. He swallowed the urge to profess his feelings. History had taught him to keep his mouth shut. One of two things would happen the minute he confessed anything. He'd get bored and want to move on, or she'd want a large diamond ring and a wedding date. It was better to say nothing. Whatever he was feeling wouldn't last long enough to ruin this moment.

Without coaxing, she unbuttoned her jeans and stepped out of them. He ran his hands along her firm outer thighs. With her head thrown back, her long regal neck invited a kiss. He planted kisses along the column. A long, slow moan escaped her throat. It sounded like a plea for him.

He eased her down on the bed and climbed on top of her. Their mouths locked in a passionate kiss that made maintaining his control harder. Pleasing her had to come first, but she reached for his hardness and the connection sent his body into a heated frenzy. He ground his hips into her and she matched each of his movements. With his hand behind her head, he lifted it slightly to deepen the kiss. Their tongues locked in a wanton dance that pushed him beyond passion. Dakota had infiltrated the barrier that kept him distant from attachment. Every moment spent with her and her uncomplicated honesty chipped at this resolve. He wanted to surrender to her and enjoy the moment. They weren't just making love, they were communicating in a way he never had before

"Let me get the condom." He reached for the foil pack on the dresser next to the bed.

She kissed his chest, then worked her way lower, running her tongue around his belly button, and then she closed her mouth over the head of his shaft. Behind his closed eyelids, the sparkling lights were hard to shut out. Her tongue traced the rim, sending blood rushing to his already-stiff member. He held a fistful of her dark curls in his hand while trying to hold back the rush of ecstasy that threatened to pull him into the abyss.

"It you don't stop right now, I don't think I can hold back another second." His voice was husky as he strained to contain himself.

"Let go." She released him just enough to responded.

The heated sensation started where her mouth touched him and spread slow and steady over him like molten lava. He tightened his hold on her as his release forged through his body, pulling every hidden emotion from him as it ripped through him in a flash of multi-colored, blinding lights.

She slowly moved back up his body, kissing every raw nerve along the way. He flipped her on her back and climbed on top. She helped him sheath his erection. As soon as she pushed the latex into place, he buried his length inside her warm crevice. Her muscles tightened around him with the strength of a vice. If this time was supposed to be about her pleasure, she wasn't making it easy for him. As he pushed deeper, she repeated his name. Her throaty enunciation faded with each thrust until she was only mumbling.

"Wrap your legs around my back," he commanded.

She complied, drawing him in deeper. Each time he eased in and out of her, she moaned, her lips pressed against his neck. In the heat of the moment, she made him feel like nothing else mattered. She ran her hands over his head until their lips locked. She slipped her tongue in and out of his mouth in time with the movement of his shaft. With her hips off the bed, she held him in place until he was ready to explode. Nothing had ever been as perfect. They made love with precision. All the empty nights and bad dates seemed pointless. What he wanted and needed was in his arms. But something held him back.

"Bishop."

"Yes, baby."

"Now." She tightened her legs, holding him in place while her body shook in succinct spasms that gripped him like a fist.

Before her body came to a stop, his body joined her in a brilliant explosion of rapture that he'd never experienced before. He collapsed on top of her and tried to catch his breath.

With her legs still cradling him, she released a breath that blew cool air across his shoulder. His body was covered in perspiration.

"That was amazing," he managed after several seconds.

"I agree. You are amazing."

He froze for a moment before rolling over next to her and closing his eyes. There it was. The tone that demanded his attention, saying she wanted more, without using those words. She poked him in the side with her finger.

"Ouch. What was that for?"

"Don't get all quiet on me. I only called you amazing. Don't worry. I'm not falling in love with you or anything like that."

§§§

Dakota turned on her side to get a better view of Bishop. If he was that skittish over the word amazing, she needed to pull back. Falling in love with him would be so easy. Every time he touched her body, she couldn't help but respond. The sincere look in his eyes when she spoke to him made her think she was the most important thing in his life. But that was what made him a playboy. He knew how to make women feel special even when they weren't.

"Aren't you going to say something?" She jabbed him in his side again to mask her humiliation. "If you don't, I'll make you listen to another letter. A longer one this time."

He half smiled and half frowned, but his eyes did not meet hers. "No, don't do that. I was hoping for something better than amazing."

"You're lying. You got quiet because you're afraid I'm going to demand something from you, like a commitment, or that we become monogamous or elope." She pushed up on her elbow to look down at him. "Believe me or not, I don't want any of those things. Like you, I only want to have a good time."

"Good to know. Now that we have an agreement, can we get back to doing amazing things?"

"Don't blow me off, Bishop. If we're going to hang out, we need to be honest with each other." She sat up and blinked her eyes, hoping he wouldn't detect the yearning on her face.

"Okay. Let me just say your pronouncement took me by surprise. But it's nothing I can't handle."

"Surely you've been complimented on your bedside manner before."

"Yeah. All the time. I just didn't expect to hear it from you." Without looking at her he used his index finger to circle her nipple. "Usually, after a few dates, women are ready for me to meet their parents."

"You don't have to worry about that." She held up her hands and flashed her palms at him. "See…no strings."

By her calculation, this was about the time he would drop her off at her house and disappear. Maybe that's what needed to happen now. Even if she didn't say the words, she was falling for him. Hard. It would have been nice for their relationship to last a year, but if it had to end, now was better than later. She was one kiss from falling in love with him and that could be a fatal mistake. There were enough disasters in her past to last her for a while. No need to add Bishop onto that heap, too.

He climbed out of bed, heading toward the bathroom. A small sheen of moisture glistened between his shoulder blades. She followed his movement until he closed the door.

She took a deep breath. No matter what, she couldn't clear her head of the image of him lying naked beside her. The look in his eyes pulling her deeper in a relationship she wasn't even sure would last another month.

He strolled back in the room and clambered back into the bed.

"Are we okay?" He pulled her into his lap. With his arms draped around her, he cradled her with such tenderness that breaking away from him would take more than just willpower. She reached for the condom on the nightstand. After opening and rolling the latex down his aroused shaft, she pushed every nagging thought out of her head and allowed desire to rule for one more night.

§§§

The quiet serenity of the night erupted with a chirp. Dakota struggled to open her eyes, but the persistent sound shook the remnants of sleep away.

She nudged Bishop. "Your cell phone is ringing. Aren't you going to answer it?"

"Huh?"

"Your cell phone," she said.

He reached for it and stared at the screen. "Shit."

"What's wrong? Did something happen?" Dakota sat up and turned on the light. Bad news always rang during the wee hours of the morning.

He huffed. "It's Sharon."

She rubbed her eyes as the name registered with her. "Sharon from earlier tonight?"

"How the hell did she get this number?" He shot her a benign look, climbed out of bed, and left the room.

From the living room, all she could hear was whispering. As hard as she tried, she couldn't slow the thumping of her heart. Is this what life with Bishop would be like? Late-night calls, secret conversations, always wondering or worrying? She stood at the side of the bed, refusing to pace or to eavesdrop. Her knees almost forgot to support her, but she forced them to be strong. Something had to be strong tonight.

The waiting was always worse. It always would be. What was only a few seconds seemed like hours before he strolled back in the bedroom without the phone.

At the edge of the bed, he stood so close the heat from his body warmed her. Their eyes locked. She tried to read his thoughts, but his dark eyes revealed nothing. His breathing was smooth and regulated. While they were just supposed to be having fun and enjoying each other, her heart had skipped over the fence that should have kept her safe. She could be so happy with him, but she couldn't share him. That was not the person she wanted to be.

He ran his tongue over his lips, but still said nothing. This was the closest he'd ever stood without touching her. The proximity sent a bolt of adrenaline through her like a rocket. She willed him to touch her flesh, but his hands remained unclenched at his side. His body was as still as the night.

"I think you better take me home." She broke the spell that held them.

Instead of stepping aside, he pulled her against his chest, holding her in place with his arms around her waist.

"It won't happen again." His words didn't give her the comfort she was sure he'd intended.

"Yes, it will. Late night calls and other women come with your territory." She pushed him away and gathered her clothes.

Chapter Thirteen

Dakota watched her first customer of the morning stroll from one row to the next without removing a single book from the shelf.

"Are you looking for something specific?" From the counter, Dakota tried to encourage her to buy a book. If business didn't turn around, the doors to Bookends would soon close. The renovation would help, but it was still weeks away from beginning.

"No. I'll know it when I see it. Thanks."

"When you're ready, Jennifer will ring your sale." Dakota nodded to Jennifer before heading back to her office. In the last few days, she'd had plenty of traffic but not many buyers.

She flopped into the padded chair behind her desk and dialed her sister. "Guess what I did this weekend?" she asked when Asa picked up the phone.

"Let me see. You curled up on the sofa with your favorite flavor of hummus and watched old movies while reading letters."

"Nope. I had a date."

"With who?"

"That new architect at Harper Enterprise. You know the one, Bishop Contee."

Asa was quiet for a moment. "I didn't know you guys were dating."

"He asked me out and I decided why not? I don't think you can call it 'dating'. I think Bishop is more of a rebound fling. It felt good to be able to laugh for a change." On purpose, she left out the part about the time they'd spent together, or how he was only fooling around with her until the next leggy lady came along.

"So he made you laugh?"

"Yes, he did. I felt like my old self. Why didn't you tell me I was becoming someone different? Old and dull. I hardly recognized myself."

"I had no idea you and Brian were in such a bad state. I knew you were moping around, but I thought it was because you missed him."

"This sounds stupid now, but you and Simeon are so happy. I thought Brian and I could be just as happy. You know—sisters married to brothers," she sighed. "The whole idea seems so corny now that I've said it aloud. What could I have been thinking?"

"Honey, you're important too. That's all behind you now. Does Bishop know he's just your rebound man?"

"I haven't said those words, but I don't think that's necessary. I know he's not ready to settle down, nor does he want anything too serious."

There was a long pause.

"Go ahead and say what's on your mind, Asa. I can feel your negative thoughts, so you might as well voice them."

"You know relationships that start out that way seldom work. Someone might get hurt and I don't want it to be my sister."

Dakota ran her fingers through her hair. Asa should have had this conversation with her weeks ago. It was already too late.

"I thought Bishop was helping you with the renovation?"

"He is. He's coming over this afternoon to discuss the final plans so we can get started. Instead of focusing on the store, I'm worried about my hair and I've checked my lip gloss three times."

"That's good, right?"

"No, it's all wrong. I think I like him more than I should, simply because I'm lonely. I might be coming off as desperate."

"Wow. Can you put my sister Dakota on the phone? This must be an imposter."

"Very funny. I can't help myself, and I don't like the way I'm behaving. I don't want to be this girl."

"Look, you've been through a lot. You can enjoy yourself. You're allowed. Why don't you come with me to New York? I'm doing a charity benefit next weekend. It can be like old times. We can shop and eat and hangout."

"I won't be any fun. You know I'll try to drag you into all the vintage and eclectic shops, and you'll try to coerce me into Barney's and Saks."

"We'll compromise. For every time I pull you into a department store, you get to pull me into any store you choose. You can even pick all the restaurants." Asa sounded excited by the prospects.

"Mmm…" Dakota hesitated. It had been ages since she'd hung out with her sister. The time away might help her sort out her life and get her priorities straight. Obviously, she had some issues. "You've got yourself a deal. When do we leave?"

Asa provided the details while she scribbled them down.

Dakota leaned back in the chair. Another pile of books awaited her attention. They seemed to multiply each night. The stories usually brought her so much joy, but not so much in the last week.

"Do you think I deserve a little romance?"

"Of course you do. If you think you stand a chance of happiness, grab hold with two hands and don't let go. Don't waste another minute."

Dakota contemplated her sister's words. Asa's advice sounded easy enough. But the churning in her stomach reminded her that relationships were never that straightforward. There was always a gully just waiting to gobble her up, and this one's name was Bishop.

"For sure Bishop is not that kind of man. He's not the settling-down type. He's the have–fun-now-and-run-buck-wild type."

"Since when have you wanted a man like that?" Asa asked.

"I wasted a year of my life. I'm making up for lost time." Dakota pulled her hair away from her face.

"I hope you know what you're doing. That doesn't sound like you."

"Have you heard from Melissa?" Dakota didn't want to hear her sister's counsel. The damage had already been done. This time she couldn't point the finger of blame at anyone but herself.

"Yes. She's coming for the opening of the community center. I'm surprised she can get away."

"There's more to her visit than she's letting on. But you know Melissa. She'll tell us about it visit when she wants us to know. Look, I better go. Bishop will be here soon and I need to check my lip gloss again."

Asa laughed before hanging up the phone.

Dakota organized the books and placed them on the shelf by category before running into the bathroom and checking her lips. After a quick glance at her teeth, she walked to the front of the store.

"She bought a book," Jennifer called from behind the register.

"Our first sale of the day and it's what, two in the afternoon?" Dakota glanced at the clock. "We won't get rich that way, will we?"

"I didn't take this job as a road to wealth." Jennifer glanced at the door. "Here comes that guy again. The one you've been waiting on all morning."

Bishop opened the door. His eyes went immediately to her sheer white shirt. His face lit up just a bit. Having his attention made her tingle. At least for now, that was enough. She tried to rein in the emotion before it overwhelmed her. Bishop was a playboy. Charm dripped too easily from his tongue to be sincere. Loneliness made her vulnerable, but jumping into the wrong relationship was just as bad.

She couldn't meet his eyes. The sooner she faced reality, the sooner she could get on with her life.

"Hey, Bishop. Come back to my office so we can go over the plans." She waved for him to follow.

She hurried behind the desk. Having the large block of wood between them gave her protection. He circled the workspace. With one hand, he cupped her waist to pull her close. The first kiss was quick, just brushing her lips. The second was slow, warm, and soft.

She pressed her palm against his chest, afraid of giving in to all the emotions. The thick muscles under his shirt felt tight. She wanted to peel back the fabric and see his magnificent body.

Dakota pulled away. "We'd better take a look at your ideas or I'll never get this place done."

His eyebrow shot up. "Okay." There was a question in his voice. "Do you want to talk about the other night?"

"No." There was no way to put into words the battle raging inside her, rehashing the events of the other night wouldn't provide any answers.

He opened his tablet without taking his eyes off her. His finger scrolled across several pages before landing on something she recognized.

He used an index finger to show how he would move shelves around and how he'd push walls back. A large window popped up on what used to be a solid wall.

"That's fantastic. I love these sketches." Dakota held her hands together. Any one of his designs had to improve business in the store.

"You have to pick one, Dakota." His tone was patient.

"You're an expert, which would you recommend?"

He flipped the page back to the first design. "This one. This design will improve the flow of the store and opens up the space. These sitting areas will make customers want to stay and read. Plus, the renovation will only take five weeks."

Instead of looking at his iPad, she focused on him. The tone of his voice changed from charming to business. She nodded.

"You're right. I like that one too." She clapped her hands. "Let's do it. How soon can we get started?"

He laughed. "It'll take a little time for me to get the drawing completed, find the right contractors, and get the permits. But I'll go as fast as I can. Especially if you'll go on another date with me."

"Whoa, that sounds like blackmail." Her heart raced. She wanted to go out with him even though she knew she shouldn't.

"It is. That's just to let you know I'm not beyond doing what I have to in order to get what I want." He pulled her into his arms. His tongue claimed her mouth like no one ever had.

Fine beads of perspiration crawled across her back. The answer to his dating question was no. The word was right there waiting for her to say. Just not today.

§§§

Dakota only took a half moment to accept his kiss, which meant the incident with Sharon had blown over. But any hesitation on her part was like a large neon warning sign. Relationships were complicated. Which explained why his father argued against them.

But the time had come to forget all the preliminary dating steps where he was expected to be only half interested in her and move to the stage where they both accepted the chemistry between them without fighting.

If Adanna could see him chasing after this natural beauty, she'd be surprised. He pulled Dakota tighter, happy to have her in his arms and to smell her fresh scent. Thoughts of getting her out of her jeans and the signature skinny top multiplied in his head. She looked like spring even though the day was overcast, cold, and the trees only had a few stubborn leaves that refused to fall.

"The work will start next week. I've got to take a short trip, but I'll check on the progress while I'm away."

"Where are you heading?"

"New York. I've got to take a look at the set for your sister's fashion show. I won't be gone long."

The color drained from her face. "Asa never mentioned you were going, too."

Too? Are you joining us?"

"She asked me this morning." Dakota fidgeted with the tablet, running her fingers across it, trying to move the pages without success.

"Don't worry. I won't crash your weekend with your sister. I'm going to inspect the set design to make sure everything is safe and meets her expectations. Then I'm out." Her left eye twitched.

"Is something wrong, Dakota? What's going on? You're acting like you don't want me to be there."

"It's not that," she paused. "Look, Bishop, I have to be honest with you. I'm the kind of person who wants to put down roots and hang around for a long time, even when I probably shouldn't. You're city and I'm country. You're music and I'm books.

You're fast paced and I'm so slow I'm behind molasses. I said I was going to try something different and I did. But this kind of lifestyle is not for me."

To get a better look at her eyes, he lifted her chin with his index finger. "I don't know what that means. You like to have fun don't you? I thought we had a great time the other night."

"We did. We do. But…but—"

He pulled her into his arms and kissed her. Her lithe body folded against him, radiating warmth through his suit jacket. After a moment she wrapped her arms around his waist, but her tongue was slow to respond.

But he had no intentions of letting her push him away. Marriage or even forever wasn't on his agenda, but neither was letting her get away. Not yet. He was still trying to figure out what he wanted. What he needed. And right now he needed time. Women who played hard to get were a novelty. But he was used to getting his way. And he wanted her.

She pulled away from him. The wild-eyed look she gave him told him he needed to slow down. This was going faster than she wanted, too.

"Why did you stop kissing me?" he asked.

Her tongue ran along her bottom lip. The gesture only made it harder to keep a distance between them.

"I'm coming off the heels of a break-up and I'm probably not thinking clearly right now. I'm not being fair to either of us."

"Since we've been seeing each other, Brian has been lurking in the corner of your mind I'm here right now. Maybe you and Brian weren't meant to be together." His tone was harsher than he intended, but the sadness that Brian had caused her was hard to accept. She deserved better. "Why do you think you did something wrong? Not every relationship ends in marriage." He placed his hands on her shoulders.

"Yeah, my head gets that, but my heart doesn't."

"Did you love him? Brian?" He steeled himself for the answer.

"No. I know you and I could date for a while and have wild sex, but I'm not a serial dater. I'm looking for longevity."

He shook his head. "I don't know if I understand that. But I'll make you a promise. I'll be honest with you. You'll know where I stand at all times. I enjoy being with you. I'd like to see where we can take this."

"This isn't an amusement ride. I just told you I put my heart in a relationship and I only want to do that if I think there is a possibility for us to go somewhere."

"Are you sure this has nothing to do with Sharon?"

"Maybe a little."

"It shouldn't. Sharon's a kook. You and I are going somewhere, if you give us a chance." He paused.

For a long moment she searched his face without saying anything, as if she had to decipher the comment.

She spread her fingers and ran them through her curls. The simple gesture seemed to relax her. The line of tension along her forehead disappeared.

"Well?" He pressed her against the counter. With his knee between her legs, he kissed her again.

"Give me a little time."

"Do you like me, Dakota?" He held the back of her neck and wrapped her silky tresses around his fingers.

"Very much." She leaned her head back, making her lips available.

"That's what I want to hear."

Chapter Fourteen

Dakota packed the last things in her overnight bag. She'd ignored Bishop's calls for the balance of the week, blaming the bookstore renovation and preparing to be away for several days, but she really needed the space. The battle between her head and heart raged on and she still hadn't chosen the winner. Maybe by now some other woman had crossed his path and he was ready to move on. Her insecurity would send any man running in the opposite direction.

Her stomach knotted with guilt for being such a coward, but she couldn't see a Dakota that would let him go, no matter how much sense it made.

She let his calls go to the recorder, then she retrieved his messages. Listening to the sound of his deep voice only made her miss him more. She couldn't pretend she wasn't falling in love with him.

Every time the door to the bookstore opened, she looked up, hoping he'd found a reason to drop by and see her. The old notion that he should pursue and claim her like a lost item wouldn't go away.

The cocoon she'd built around her life was her safety net. Right now nothing was going to break through, not even the suave and debonair Bishop Contee. All she had to do was get through the weekend in New York with him hanging on the fringes. Asa would be her excuse if her resolve weakened—she wouldn't leave her sister stranded.

From the double window in her living room, she watched the limousine pull up in front of the townhouse. This trip was supposed to be fun, but she felt herself slipping backwards, like before, hardly daring to enjoy life.

As the driver loaded her bag into the trunk, she climbed in the back-seat. Asa was in the far corner with the mobile phone pushed to her ear, giving instructions on a design. While waiting for Asa to end her call, Dakota ticked off her checklist in her head. All book orders had been placed and Jennifer was in charge of the store, even though she'd frowned when Dakota gave her the list of responsibilities. But Jennifer frowned a lot lately, most often when Bishop was in the store.

In three short weeks, Bishop had shaken her life loose from its moorings. As much as she wanted to ignore him, he popped into her head at the most unexpected times. While eating breakfast, or stacking books, obscene dreams of him fueled a desire in her that simmered liked hot coals. He touched her skin with the knowledge of a lifelong lover. Her body responded to him on sight, like an out-of-control child.

Brian and Bishop were as different as David and Goliath. Brian wanted to take on the challenges of the world. Bishop seemed content to take her on. His soft, easy manner had lured her into his arms without much protest. As much as she liked Bishop, something said to keep him away from her heart. The man was a womanizer. She saw the way women looked at him, like he was a feast for the eyes.

Asa ended her call and squealed. "Sorry about that. There's a problem with some of the fabric I ordered." She leaned over and gave Dakota a squeeze. "I'm so glad you agreed to come with me."

"I didn't know we were being chauffeured to New York. This is nice."

"I figured you needed a treat."

Dakota pressed her hand into the soft leather seat. "I could get used to this kind of treatment."

"Well don't. We might catch the train home. It depends how well the show goes."

"You're always so modest." Dakota grabbed her sister's arm. "You've arrived. I'm surprised you're still resisting it."

"I never want to take my happiness for granted. It's a gift and I'm blessed to have Simeon and Mia."

"What will Simeon and Mia do without you for two nights?"

"Simeon won't miss my granny panties and nursing bra for a couple of nights." Asa laughed.

"Are you kidding me? Simeon misses you when you're gone for a few minutes." Dakota was quiet for several moments. "Do you think I'll ever find the person that's right for me like you and Melissa have?"

"Sure you will. Mim said there's a lid for every pot and I believe it. You'll know when he comes along." Asa patted her sister's hand, her gold bangles jingled with each stroke.

"Why did you invite Bishop to work on your set? Of all the architects who work for Harper Enterprise, couldn't you find someone else?"

Asa made the shape of an O with her mouth. Her brain seemed to be searching for an answer. "I didn't think about it. Simeon assigned him.

He'll meet us for lunch. As soon as we go over the design, he should be able to leave. Is that going to be a problem for you?"

Dakota pushed her curls off her forehead. "That's fine. He's here to work with you, not me. Besides, I think after this week, he got my message."

"What did you do, Dakota?" Asa enunciated each word.

"Nothing, I'm just avoiding him, that's all." She rubbed her thumbs together. "Has Simeon heard from Brian?"

"I don't think so. He's at some outpost somewhere in Central America. He's probably living in a tent."

"Do you think he's ever coming back to Bristol?"

"Why? Do you want him to?"

"I do. Not because I want a relationship. There are just some things that I never got to say. We have unfinished business. I know this phrase is overused, but I need closure." The word coated her mouth with distaste.

"You don't want to strangle him, do you?"

"Maybe a little." She measured with her thumb and index finger.

"So, about Bishop. What's going on?" Asa held her gaze.

"Bishop isn't Mr. Right, he's Mr. Right Now. Extending the relationship isn't good for either of us. I'm lonely and he likes to have fun. That's a recipe for disaster."

Asa nodded. For the balance of the drive Asa regaled her with stories about baby Mia's antics.

Asa shook Dakota's shoulder just as they emerged from the Lincoln Tunnel Dakota peered out the window at the mob of people and the activity on Manhattan streets. She enjoyed watching people, and the limousine with its darkened window provided the perfect cover. Traffic crawled as they neared West 44th Street. The car eased to a stop in front of the Hotel Sofitel. Before she could grab her knapsack, the doorman opened the door.

They were escorted to a two-room suite. A bouquet of flowers graced the coffee table.

"These must be from Simeon," Asa gushed. "How sweet." She pulled the card free from the white calla lilies and looked at the envelope.

"They're for you," she said.

"Me? Who would…?"

Asa handed her the note with a smile and disappeared into one of the bedrooms. "Maybe you have a secret admirer," she called over her shoulder.

Dakota slid the card from the envelope. "Have a good weekend. I'll give you as much time as you need." The writing on the card was scripted in a flowery pattern that couldn't be Bishop's. She held the card close to her chest. He promised one thing, but he was hard to tune out. The last time she'd received flowers had to be as a corsage for her high school prom.

She tucked the card into the pocket of her jeans and carried the flowers into the opposite bedroom. From her bag, she removed the sage-filled satchel and lit the end with a match. She waved it around her room before moving into the living area.

"Do you want me to cleanse the aura of your room?" she asked her sister before entering her bedroom.

Asa rolled her eyes toward the ceiling, but nodded.

"I know you think this is a waste of time, but it makes me feel better." She walked around the king-sized bed, waving the satchel in the air.

"That's why I'm not going to complain. When you're done, let's grab some lunch. I'm hungry."

Dakota knew her sister thought she was a scatterbrain, but she had to honor the old soul that dwelled inside of her. While Asa unpacked, Dakota continued to cleanse the suite.

"Are you changing for lunch?" Asa stuck her head in the bedroom.

Dakota looked down at her tight jeans and knee-high suede boots, then at her sister's off-white wool slacks and matching cashmere crew neck sweater. "What's wrong with what I'm wearing? You're here on business, this is pleasure for me."

"Just checking is all. Bishop is meeting us to go over the design."

Dakota ran her hand through her hair. "Uh," she sighed. "Maybe I shouldn't go. I can meet you here after you're done."

"Don't even think about ditching." Asa pulled her arm. "You're going."

Bishop was already seated at the table when they arrived in the dining room. Asa took the seat across from him leaving the chair next to him open. He held the chair out for Dakota.

"How are you?" he whispered close to her ear. She hadn't heard his voice in days and his question sounded like a sonnet.

She wanted to say something that was just as seductive, something that would make him as needy as he made her, something that made his body tingle all over, but her tongue got stuck and wouldn't cooperate. "I'm good."

Hunger pains fought with the anxiety in her stomach for center stage as she sat down. By the time the server showed up to take their orders, Dakota was ready to eat the menu.

Bishop placed his ever-ready tablet on the table. While he and Asa reviewed the designs for the set, she watched the other patrons, trying to pretend Bishop's proximity had no impact on her. His thigh pressed against her leg. He had to be doing it on purpose. The large rectangular table had plenty of room. The wave of desire that emanated from his touch was exhilarating to her. She sipped her glass of ice water, hoping for some relief.

"Dakota, you're awfully quiet. I hope this shop talk isn't boring you," Asa said.

"You two go right ahead. I'm fine."

"So what's on the agenda for this afternoon?" Bishop directed his question to Dakota.

She folded her arms on the table and looked at her sister. "We haven't decided yet. We're going to do some shopping, of course."

Asa's phone rang. As she reached for it, Bishop turned to her. "Good to see you, Dakota. As always, you look fantastic."

"As always, you're just being nice. But thanks." Dakota patted her hair which she hadn't combed since leaving room

Asa ended her call. "Dakota, you're going to kill me. But as soon as we're done here I need to slip out for a few hours to talk with my design assistant. She couldn't resolve the fabric dilemma. I shouldn't be long. I promise."

"Don't worry —"

"Maybe Bishop can keep you company until I come back."

Dakota ignored the pitying look in her sister's eyes. The little witch in Dakota's head said her sister had set up the phone call just so she could leave her with Bishop. Alone. But she snapped her mouth shut.

Bishop studied Dakota's face while she watched her sister hurry out the door. Tension etched her jaw, but she was still the most attractive woman in the room. Her full pouty lips glistened from her favorite lip gloss. He could hear his father calling him a chump for being so drawn to her, willing to give anything for her acceptance.

"It's not so bad, me being here, is it?" he asked.

She took a short breath. "I just feel like this was set-up."

"Well, I didn't do it. But I like the opportunity to talk to you. You've been avoiding me."

"I explained my position the last time we talked. There are more reasons for us to go our separate ways than there are for us to be together." She rested her chin in her palm, her dark eyes penetrated his.

"I don't believe that."

"Look, we're in New York. There are hundreds maybe thousands, of beautiful women here who would love to hang out with you. Since you and

Asa are done with your business, why don't you go have a blast? You don't need to keep me company."

The tension in her face eased. Maybe getting that off her chest was like putting down a heavy load. Pursuing Dakota began as a challenge. Now being with her was a necessity. In the week since she stopped taking his calls, it only accentuated how much he needed and missed her.

The server cleared the empty dishes. Bishop signed the check and pushed the black pouch to the center of the table.

"I won't compete with your ex, Dakota, or ghosts of boyfriends past."

"What ghost? There isn't anyone else."

"Sure there is. You say you didn't love Brian, but you're acting as if you owe him something. Like you're in mourning and can't get on with another relationship until a respectful amount of time has passed. You know that's all bullshit, don't you?"

"It would be bullshit if anything you just said was true. My feelings about you and I have nothing to do with Brian. You see that woman over there drooling over you?" She nodded her chin across the room. "I don't want to compete with that every day. Sooner or later you're going to miss all that action."

He reached for her hand, holding on tight. "I never asked you to. You aren't competing with anyone."

They sat in silence for several moments, staring at each other.

Without releasing her hand, he stood.

"Where are we going?" she asked as he led her out of the dining room.

In the middle of the hotel lobby, he leaned in so close he could feel the softness of her breast on his arm. Her rosy scent caused an explosion of desire through his body. "I have an idea. Two, actually. We can go to my room, or we can visit the Guggenheim. Which do you choose?" he whispered in her ear, just for an excuse to get closer.

She turned her head so that her lips were almost touching his. "I've already seen the exhibit at the Guggenheim." Her tone was the most seductive he'd ever heard.

Chapter Fifteen

The elevator doors opened. It might have been easier to let his hand go and walk into the empty car, but she couldn't, or she'd float away. The moment was like magic, she didn't want to break the spell and let reality snatch the feeling away.

Her stomach jiggled like a whacky washing machine with an uneven load. She took a shallow breath through her nose and released a puff of air through her mouth. Then she did it again, hoping Bishop couldn't see how nervous she was. His dark eyes smoldered with desire.

When the elevator doors closed, he pinned her in the corner. With his hands resting on her hips, he held her gaze.

"I missed you." His voice had a way of drawing out the bad girl in her. Being responsible and sensible was highly overrated. The only thing that made any sense right now was being with him.

"Let me see how much." She reached for his crotch. His stiff shaft expanded through the fine wool fabric of his pants and filled her hand.

"You know there are hidden cameras in here. Someone can see everything you're doing." He glanced up toward the ceiling.

"I don't care. They might see something that will brighten their day."

"I know I have."

The bell rang as the car came to a stop. They nearly ran to his room at the end of the hall. His key card didn't work the first time.

"Maybe if you take your hand off my butt, you could get the door unlocked." Dakota threw her hip against his.

The second time he pulled the key through the slot slower and the green light came on. Together they tumbled inside the room. He kicked the door closed with his foot while pulling her shirt over her head.

"Are you sure about this? I don't want another fire drill. Either you're in or you're out." He ran his thumb across her cheek.

"Shhh. Please don't ask me a lot of questions. All I know is that right now I want you more than I ever wanted anything. I don't want to overthink this moment. I just want to enjoy it."

He pulled off his jacket and threw it on a nearby stuffed chair. "I want to grant your wish."

She unbuttoned his shirt to expose the most exquisite six pack she'd ever seen that wasn't on the pages of a magazine. Bishop was storybook perfect, but fairytales always came to an end. The point was to enjoy this moment, and she planned to do just that.

Every inch of him looked marvelous. She didn't want to think about being without him. It might be foolish to keep returning to the rollercoaster, but she was hooked.

He trailed his index finger along her jaw, down her neck to her collarbone. The light touch ignited a slow burn at the base of her spine.

He gave her a peck on the lips, and then captured her mouth, drawing her tongue into a slow sexy tango. The slightly salty taste of his tongue was delicious. If there were academy awards for kissing, Bishop would receive the golden statue.

He unsnapped her jeans and wiggled them down her legs. "With these gorgeous legs, you should wear shorts up to here." He drew a line on her upper thigh that ended between her legs.

"That might be fine for the bedroom, but not the bookstore."

"Then I'll just have to keep you in the bedroom." He picked her up and carried her to the bed. He climbed between her legs and resumed the kiss.

Relishing his touch, smell, and taste, she planted kisses on his neck as she tried to absorb every inch of him. Her exhilaration from the elevator shifted into high gear. She wanted him. His rod throbbed against her leg. She caressed the warm shaft, moving her hand up the shaft as she rotated her hips.

"Tell me you have condoms in your wallet." The deep, lusty timbre of her voice sounded foreign to her ears. A new side of her emerged whenever he came within five feet. All she needed to do was to find a way to get him to stay forever.

He smiled down at her. The intense look in his eyes wrecked her resolve. Nothing could compare to the pleasure coursing through her body in that moment. While remaining on top of her, he reached into his wallet and produced a condom. She slid from under him to help him undress. His pants hit the floor with a loud clang.

"My keys," he said as he removed his briefs.

Dakota opened the sheath and tugged it into place. She straddled him, squatting to guide him into her. The moment he filled her, she almost uttered the three little words that would turn her world inside out. Instead, she locked her mouth over his. Maybe her tongue could convey what her mind wouldn't allow her to say.

She drilled her hips into him until she couldn't withhold the mounting pressure building in her veins. As she writhed above him, he released his passion, too. She was going to try to play this game for as long as her soul allowed. He was just too good to walk away from.

§§§

He held her in the crease of his arm, not quite sure what to say. One wrong word and she might scurry beyond his reach. He'd half expected her to smack him when he suggested they come to his room, instead she'd accepted. Just when he thought he knew Dakota and what she wanted, she changed direction.

Without opening her eyes, she ran her finger up and down his chest, flipping from one side of her finger to the other. He picked up her hand and placed her index finger in his mouth. The low, long moan that slipped past her lips was almost inaudible. He cupped a breast. Her nipples were the color of newly minted pennies. Her skin was soft so he lightened his touch, careful not to bruise her. Propped on one elbow, he sucked her nipple, imagining having this pleasure every day for the rest of his life. The tip hardened under the pressure of his tongue. As he moved to place kisses on her breastbone, she arched her back off the bed, pressing against him. With his palm flat against her abdomen, she grabbed his shaft and squeezed.

This was more than the casual sex he was used to. In the short time he'd known Dakota, she'd inched under his skin, invading places where no one was allowed. The last thing he needed was a real girlfriend. The first thing he wanted was Dakota. Any way she'd have him. He slipped his finger into her wet folds. The movement seemed to jerk her body involuntarily. She wrapped her leg over his and pulled him closer.

"Just a minute." He leaned off the bed and patted the floor for his wallet. With one hand he flipped it over and extracted another sheath. Together, they rolled it on.

He gripped the headboard for support as he pushed into her. Every muscle in her lower body contracted, increasing the intensity on his manhood. He ached for her and had to harness his pent-up desire. He didn't want to rush this moment. Making his movements slow and concentrated took every ounce of energy he could muster as she repeated his name in a raspy voice. The sound heightened his need for her. He wanted to please her, to take her to a place that would become special for them.

The throaty harmony of her voice vibrated in his ear as she tightened her legs around him. The rotation of her hips increased. "I'm coming, now, Bishop." It sounded like a command and his body responded. The contractions of her muscles against his hardness set off an explosion that bloomed through his body, leaving him limp and spent.

He gasped for air. She panted softly beside him while staring at the ceiling. Her lips formed the most beautiful pout he'd ever seen.

"What is it? You're nearly frowning."

"I was thinking. I don't believe I'm in your hotel room, in your bed. Perfectly naked."

"I agree. You're perfect."

She swatted his arm. "I'm serious. You wouldn't believe how many times I said this was not going to happen."

"You're not going to say this was a mistake, are you?"

"Why would I say that?" She pushed up and looked at him.

"That only happens in movies. I'm more like a puppy. Feed me and I'll hang around forever."

"Oh, yeah."

"I was only joking. I don't want you to think I'm some stalker chick." She kissed him.

"I think you've got me all wrong," he said.

"Shhh. We don't need to dissect this." She swung her legs off the edge of the bed.

He glanced at the clock on the table beside the bed. "It's not too late to go to the Guggenheim. We can still catch part of the exhibit."

"Maybe some other time." She climbed out of the bed.

The curtains were still open. It wasn't too dark outside, but the neon lights from Time Square brightened the room. With her round rump exposed, she picked up her clothes from the floor.

"Are you leaving?"

"I think I'd better. I need to get back to the room to meet Asa."

He jumped out of bed and pulled on his pants. "Let me ride with you upstairs."

She held up her hand to stop him. "No. You stay here. Please."

Chapter Sixteen

Dakota darted into the suite and shed her clothes as she ran to the shower. Her jeans, her top, her shoes, but she held onto Bishop's essence. It clung to her like a mist of cologne. The giddy feeling she'd felt on the way to New York intensified. How can something she wanted so much be bad for her?

As she lathered, the play-by-play details of the afternoon popped in her head. The way he touched her body confirmed that she was desirable to someone. She could have made love to him all day long. But pacing was important, otherwise she could fly away like a runaway kite. She hummed as she rinsed he suds from her body and stepped out.

By the time Asa walked in the suite, Dakota was stretched across one of the chairs with a book in her hand. She hadn't read one word on the page. Instead, she relished the happiness that kept shocking her heart and making her smile.

"Sorry about that. I hope I wasn't gone too long." Asa dropped her purse on the floor and plopped in the chair beside her. She swung her legs over the arm of the chair.

"Not at all. I found something to keep me busy." The words sounded more coy than she intended.

"Something or someone?" Her sister grinned.

"I won't kiss and tell." Dakota closed the book and sat up straight.

"So, there was kissing going on, huh? It appears you're no longer pining over—"

Dakota held up her hand. "Don't even say his name. If I never hear his name again that's fine with me. I've moved on." Lying to Asa wasn't something she liked to do, but there was no way to explain what was going on in her head to her sister.

"Okay. Don't get your britches in a knot." She swung her foot. A wrinkle appeared between her brows. "Do you think you should get involved with Bishop?"

"Why are you asking me that? Do you know something?"

"You and Brian just broke up. I think you're rebounding, which isn't fair to you or to Bishop."

"I'm a big girl, Asa." Dakota crossed her arms around her waist.

"I worry about you. No matter how you felt about Brian, that breakup impacted you."

"I'm not thinking about a long-term relationship. Not right now. After a yearlong lull, I deserve to have some fun?"

"You're not a have-fun kind of person. Either you'll get hurt or you'll end up fighting with Bishop. Nobody wins if you go into a relationship using him to fill your heartbreak."

Dakota stood up and placed her hands on her hips. "I'm not in a relationship with Bishop and I'm not using him. I'm having some fun and that's all he wants, too. I'm lonely, Asa. I've spent the last year talking to myself, eating alone, and going to bed alone and having sex alone. I want someone to talk to late at night when you're cuddled up with your husband. Bishop is a grown man. I haven't made any promises to him and I don't plan to."

Asa stood too. "I'm not judging you, Dakota. I just want you to slow down and think about what you're doing." The sideways glance she gave Dakota was loaded with warning.

"I'm always thinking about what I'm doing. I've spent the last year with nothing but time to think. Look what thinking got me, Asa. Nothing." The high pitch of her voice strained her throat.

Asa placed her hand on Dakota's shoulders. "I'm just worried about you. No matter what, I'll be here for you." Asa gave her arm a squeeze.

"Thanks, but let me just do this my way. If I need you, I promise I'll let you know.

Asa shook her head. "Look, this is supposed to be a fun weekend. So, are you ready to hit the streets? Should we shop first or sightsee first?"

Dakota curled a lock of hair around her finger. "Let's shop. I hear a pair of shoes calling my name."

Asa looked at her watch. "I'm not meeting Bishop until six. We can do a lot of damage before then."

"Let's go." Dakota made her way to the door.

§§§

Four hours later, they pushed their bags into the back seat of the cab and climbed in.

"That was so much fun. I haven't been shopping for anything nice and sexy since the baby was born." Asa opened the Saks' bag and pulled out the box. "Don't you love these Manolos?"

Dakota nodded. "They're nice, if you want to spend all day in five-inch heels."

Asa dropped them back in the bag and sighed. "I'm exhausted. I'm not used to all this running around." She put the bag at her feet. "Do you want to stop at the hotel or do you want to go with me to the center for my meeting?"

Dakota pretended to think about her options. "I'll tag along."

"We won't be long." Asa yawned.

§§§

Bishop stood in front of the hall in his signature trench coat and suit. Dakota scrutinized him. When did she fall in love with such a traditional man? Desk job, business suits, straight nine to-five. His bad-boy appeal was the only thing outside the mold. She figured her man would be the outdoor type, who liked hunting, fishing, or counting stars. Did that mean she'd start wearing gray slacks and white button down blouses?

His handsome silhouette looked amazing. Dakota caught her breath. She hardly recognized herself. She was acting like a high school girl going to the prom. She wanted was a repeat of their afternoon. Even a small slice of their earlier tryst would make her sing happy songs for days.

She didn't recognize herself and for now that was okay. As long as she didn't fall back into what she was used to, maybe she'd be okay. Bishop helped them out of the cab and held the bags. He led the way into the hall, gesturing right and left, pointing out things he'd already taken care of, while their packages swung from his arms like appendages. No matter which side of the set Dakota stood on, he managed to sidle next to her. The simple gesture sent her confidence soaring ten points. If she ever got him in bed again, she'd have to give him a special thank you.

He placed their shopping bags on the floor and turned on his tablet. While he discussed the required changes, Dakota moved away from them.

The wrinkle in her sister's brow returned.

"Maybe I should go back to the room and let you guys talk business," Dakota said, moving toward the door. This was supposed to be a business trip for Asa, not an opportunity for her to frolic with Bishop.

"I think we're almost done here." Bishop closed the lid on his trusty tablet. "Asa, if you're okay with these changes, the contractor will make them first thing in the morning well before the show.”

“They’re perfect.” She released a big breath. “Dakota, are you ready to call it a night?”

“Dakota, do you mind if I speak to you for a minute? Let me buy you a drink.” His eyes pinned her for an answer. Dakota looked from her sister to Bishop. She felt like the rope in a tug of war. She opened her mouth, and then closed it again.

“You go ahead, Dakota. I want to call home and talk to Simeon before it gets too late.” She picked up her bags.

“Are you sure?”

“I am, sweetie.” She kissed Dakota’s cheek. “Have a good night.”

As Dakota made her way to the exit, Bishop slipped his hand into hers

“You didn’t think we were finished, did you?” he asked when they were alone.

“Not by a long shot.” She stretched on her toes and kissed him. “What have you got in mind?”

“I should probably take you to a nice club or a show. But I’ve got wine chilling in my room. I stopped at the Duane Reade for more condoms, and I've got your name tattooed on my brain."

"Then what are we waiting for?"

Chapter Seventeen

Bishop rolled up the drawings and shoved them in the desk drawer. Life just kept getting better. Forget that garbage Dad had spewed about being young and wild. He was where he wanted to be and with the woman he wanted to be with. This time last week he was entangled in the soft cotton sheets of his hotel suite with Dakota. Her curvy, petite body was just as fiery in bed as it was out. Talking to her was just as much fun as bedding her.

He rubbed his finger across his chin and tried to push away the memories. He didn't want to spend all his time thinking about her, but she kept coming to mind. Her soft touch, her smell, or just the way she whispered his name. The last thing he needed was to focus so much time on her. This was the kind of thing that had guys buying rings and thinking of cute ways to propose marriage. His brothers and father would call him a chump if they knew of his emotional attachment to Dakota.

Happily ever after was not his reality. Based on his calculations, he still had eight years before even considering settling down. There was only one thing wrong with his plan. No other woman had even crossed his mind since he met Dakota.

He dialed her number, anxious to hear her voice.

"What's up?" he asked when she answered the phone.

"Hey babe." She'd started using the affectionate term the day they returned from New York. He wasn't sure if it was the blow your-mind sex or if she'd mentally moved him out of the friend zone into that special category. Either way, he liked where they were

"Do you need me to pick up anything before coming by?" He was careful not to say home, even though he'd slept there every night this week.

"You've eaten vegetarian almost every night this week, how about a nice, big, juicy steak?"

"Are you serious? You wouldn't tease a brother, would you?"

"I would, but not about this," she laughed.

"I was thinking we could do something special tonight."

"That's sounds ominous. Special like what?" she purred into the phone.

"I want you to meet my baby sister and her family. How about dinner at her place?"

"Mmm. I don't think that's such a good idea."

"Dinner wouldn't be anything special. It's not like you're meeting my mother or anything. I just need a buffer between me and my brother-in-law."

"I'm sure you can handle your brother-in-law. You have a way with people. Besides you've gotten along with him without me all this time."

"I haven't. I keep a lot of distance between me and him."

"So, what am I now?"

"You seem to be everything I need. You said you wanted to meet my sister. Now's the time."

"Okay," she responded slowly. "What time?"

"I'm on my way. I'll pick you up at your house. I'm leaving the office right now. But one night this week I still want that steak you promised." He hung up and ran his hands down his face. Every day, he promised himself to back away a little from her and every day he went directly to her house as soon as he was finished in the office.

The best part of his waking hours was only minutes away. He picked up his briefcase and dashed toward the elevator.

She opened the door as soon as he rang the doorbell. Even though she kept a key taped in the bottom of the mailbox, he refused to let himself in. When she placed the key in the palm of his hand, then he'd really feel welcome.

Tonight her hair fell in soft curls to her shoulders. Her big smile said she was as happy to see him as he was to see her.

Without saying a word, he kissed her. They had their own language. He only hoped he understood her unspoken words. Her mouth was warm and minty. He cupped her neck to pull her closer while enjoying her tongue. After several moments, she placed her palms flat on his chest as she released him.

"Bishop, it's been a week. You practically live here now. When are you going to start using the key?" she asked.

"Practically is a long way from the real thing."

"You have a toothbrush in my bathroom and I'm sure I saw your sexy, silk boxers in the hamper the other day."

That's how it began. First some toiletries, then a few pieces of clothing, then the freedom that was his prize since he was old enough to clench his fist. If this game of tug of war between his wants and what he was taught didn't resolve itself soon, he knew his heart would step in and set the direction. And it would be right here.

"We can go see my sister another night."

She lifted an eyebrow. "Oh, no. We're going to see your sister. I've hyped myself up for this visit and we need to do it while I still have the courage."

He held the door open for her. "My family really isn't that bad. Well, maybe my mother is, but that's another story. My father is more of an epic drama. It takes a lifetime to figure him out, so good luck with that. But, I'm not so sure I want to share you tonight."

She patted his hand. "I promise I'll give you my undivided attention when we get home."

§§§

Dakota rubbed her hands together. Traffic should have been as thick as fog to slow them down and give her time to think about this visit. Instead, Bishop zipped through town and on to Limestone

Road within minutes. Her mind tried to weave more into the invitation than he'd ever implied. Meeting his parents didn't mean a walk down the aisle.

Without wanting to, she couldn't stop making mental plans for their future. Her thoughts ran headstrong into a blizzard in bare feet. Only this time, her heart was exposed. The feeling was wonderful and scary all at the same time.

They were ticking along just fine. The store was under construction. He was spending more time at her house than at his place, and life was good. Throwing family and expectations into the mix was sure to throw off their equilibrium.

"Why are you fidgeting? My sister is great. You'll like her. You might even be a good influence on her.

"Do you normally introduce your girlfriends to your family?"

He didn't answer right away. Instead, he tapped the steering wheel and tried to shift lanes.

"Well, do you?"

"No. But I don't have many long-term relationships."

"We haven't been together that long. Four weeks doesn't count as long term, Bishop."

"To me, four weeks means more than you can image."

"I see. For a playboy, four weeks must sound like an eternity." She shifted in her seat to stare at him. The conversation made him feel a little uncomfortable now.

"I wouldn't call myself a playboy. I like you. It's as simple as that."

"Nothing is ever as simple as it seems. I found that out the hard way." Her voice was flat, she worked hard to keep her emotions out of the conversation.

Bishop turned left onto Paper Mill Road without looking at her. The conversation must have made him uncomfortable. Good.

"Tell me about Adanna and Dennis."

"Let's see. She came to the East Coast to get her degree at Drexel. Instead, Dennis got her pregnant. At least he married her, but he barely supports her or the baby."

"You sound as if your sister had no say in any of the things that happened to her. What happened can't be all Dennis's fault."

He turned into a housing development with a mixture of townhouses and single-family homes and came to a stop in front of a three-story brick townhouse.

"She wasn't ready to get married or have a family. Now she's trying to make the best of a bad situation. And the fact that my parents don't approve doesn't help. They haven't even seen their newest grandchild yet. My mother refuses to come for a visit."

"Life happens to everyone. You can't always control the turns or twists." She had proof of that. He hadn't been part of her life script. She'd thought her future was supposed to be built around Brian. But that was long before he decided what he wanted wasn't found on American soil.

"Are you the go-between for your mother and your sister?"

"My family is important to me. I feed my mother info on my sister and send her pictures. My parents finally agreed to come to the community center opening for me."

"That's next week!" Her heartbeat doubled. He'd dropped that piece of information as if he was reading a store flyer. But the car felt like it was spinning. She grabbed the door handle to steady her out of control world.

"Yeah, but don't mention any of this to Adanna. It's a surprise."

"It's a surprise to me, too. You are full of them. Were you planning to tell me your parents were coming to town? If she's going to the opening, I'll see her."

"Slow down, Dakota. She just agreed to come today. So what if you meet my mother?" He shrugged.

"Family involvement is always more complicated than you think. Trust me."

Chapter Eighteen

Dakota managed to get through dinner with his family—she was as pleasant as he promised. But thinking about meeting his parents caused her heart to bounce around in a constant rush of hiccups. She adjusted her seatbelt and exhaled a long breath. Every minute she spent with Bishop was like waking up on Christmas morning and finding everything you wanted under the tree. Meeting his sister had turned out better than she'd expected, so meeting his parents had to be the scene when the Grinch arrived and snatched everything back.

Having both of her parents killed suddenly had only cemented the idea in her mind that life was full of surprises. Having your boyfriend breakup with you by way of a cassette tape did little to dispel the belief. Even Mim's sage clichés didn't help put her back together again. Some scars took longer to heal, but she had to stop picking at the wound.

Bishop drove with one hand and held hers with the other.

"That wasn't so bad, was it?" he asked as the townhouse faded through the rear window.

"Dinner with your family was fun. Your sister is sweet. I can see why you adore her." She stroked the top of his hand. "Next week is what worries me."

"Don't. My parents are just people. They don't run my life. Never have. I make my own decisions."

"Will you tell them you're spending most of your nights at my place?"

"Have you told your sisters?"

She shook her head.

"Why not? Why don't you want them to know?" He glanced at her quickly then returned his eyes to the road.

"What's to tell them? They know we're seeing each other, beyond that, I don't know if I can even define what's going on." She paused. "Anyway, I'll just wait and see where we go before I start telling people."

He parked the car in front of her house and turned off the ignition. "What does that mean? You sound like this is some kind of test I have to pass before you can tell anyone about me."

With the engine off, the cold seeped in. She shivered. "I'm freezing. We better go inside before my teeth start chattering."

He grabbed her arm. "Not until you answer my question. Is this a test?" His eyes narrowed and darkened.

"Bishop, you're a womanizer. I don't expect you to change your stripes any time soon. You've said as much. So let's not pretend this is something it's not. We're having fun. I'm trying to accept what our relationship is." She kissed his cheek. "Let's not tarnish what we have."

"Is that what this is for you? Just fun? Maybe it's not me that's holding us back. You've got some issues of your own."

She looked at him for a long time, trying to erase the mental images of him with his arm linked with the blond bombshell or some other beauty in a tangle of arms and legs while he moaned her name. "Maybe I do." she managed to say.

§§§

Bishop was pleased with the way her body had responded to his touch, but her mind had been occupied with something other than the pleasure he tried to give her. Sometime during the night, she'd inched away from him and curled around the pillow.

Clouds blocked the daylight as the sun crossed the horizon. A gray haze crept into the room, providing just enough brilliance for him to see her face. The tension between her brows was gone. He pulled her closer and held her like a precious gift. As much as he wanted to deny his feelings for her, he couldn't fool himself. Not anymore.

"Are you awake?" she asked him.

"Just barely. I didn't sleep much last night since you decided to stay on the far side of the bed." He stroked her shoulders.

"I saw your sister pull you into the kitchen last night. I'm smart enough to know she wanted to talk about me. So what did she say? Did I pass the test?"

"How did you know that?" He squeezed her.

"It's a woman thing. What did she say?"

"She really liked you. She says you're different."

"Different how? Good or bad?"

"All good. You're my unique beauty." He nuzzled his nose into the curve of her neck and took a deep breath.

"Are you smelling me?" She giggled.

"For a start." He kissed each breast. Her soft, warm skin felt good to touch. He trailed his finger down her breastbone and slid his finger into her wet core. She arched off the bed, capturing his mouth.

While playing with her tongue, she stroked his chest, his abdomen, his thighs, then she gripped his rod. The gentle massage made it hard to concentrate. His senses were primed to burst. Dakota was more than just someone to have a good time with. He wanted a life with her. The thought made him catch his breath.

He shifted away from her touch to kiss her belly button. He rolled his tongue over her stomach and between her legs. What had started out as fun was now something much more significant. As her moans echoed in his head, all he wanted to do was please her—and not only in bed.

"Oh, Bishop," she repeated his name. Her body stiffened and she gripped his ears. After her body collapsed into the mattress, she continued to whisper his name.

"Yes," he responded

"You're fabulous."

"You're just saying that because you want more.

She nodded.

The room fell quiet. She was sprawled across the king-sized bed with her hands above her head. He pulled open the bedside drawer and removed a condom. After he put it on, he kissed his way to her lips and slid his tongue inside her mouth. She wrapped her lean legs around him and rotated her hips, drawing him into her depth.

"You are something else," he muttered in her ear.

"We're a perfect pair."

The truthfulness in her words reverberated in his head. He shut it out as he matched her rhythm. The sweet connection between their bodies was like one of those old love songs from his teenage years. He released the bonds that kept him from concentrating on the luxury of her body. Slipping in and out of her as her muscles contracted around his shaft sent heat rising up his spine and drove him deeper. When he couldn't resist the mounting pressure a moment longer, his body shook as an explosion of ecstasy coursed through every vein of his body.

When his breathing returned to normal, he rolled beside her with his arm still draped over her stomach. Being with her was so natural. No pretending required. He didn't have to make conversation or entertain her.

"I better get to the bookstore to prepare for renovation." She moved to the edge of the bed.

He pulled her tighter, not ready to let her go, yet. Something held him back. He wasn't ready to settle down, but Dakota was as close as he'd ever gotten. There was a warm feeling in his heart whenever she was around. Something he wanted to hold on to forever and protect. But he couldn't form the words. Not yet.

With his hand under the soft mound of her left breast, he tried to feel her heartbeat. After a few seconds, her pulse pumped against his palm. Each faint beat traveled through his veins to his heart, as if joining them together.

He climbed out of bed. "I better get out of here. This is going to be a busy week. I'll drop by Bookends later in the week to help you get ready for the contractors." He reached for his pants and caught a glimpse of her over his shoulder. "I'm picking my parents up at the airport on Monday, so I might be busy while they're in town. You know, playing referee between them and my sister." The statement wasn't entirely true, but maybe a little space would help him sort out what was happening. He certainly couldn't think straight while spending every available minute with Dakota.

She reached for her panties beside the bed, giving him a divine view of her perfect ass.

"Melissa is coming into town for the opening this week too. We'll both be swamped in family activity."

She didn't look at him as she made her way to the bathroom.

Chapter Nineteen

Dakota rounded the corner of Bookends and hunched her shoulders against the wind. After two days of having Melissa as a houseguest, the walk to the store was refreshing. The next time she saw Darius, she'd remind him he owed her a small fortune for giving him a reprieve from his bossy wife.

Dashing from one store to another to find Melissa the right dress, then the perfect shoes, followed by the most exquisite French dinner available in Delaware, she still found time to miss Bishop, but she was determined to adjust to the condition. Living without him could be permanent in an instant.

Bishop leaned against the front door of Bookends. Dressed in jeans and a sweatshirt, he was hardly recognizable. His rugged appearance held a smidge more appeal than his male-model persona. In his casual attire, he looked like a bad boy.

Her stomach flopped on its side as his big smile greeted her. He balanced a large box of donuts in his palm and his briefcase sat at his feet. He held the box out to her like a peace offering when she walked up.

"I wasn't expecting you this early." She unlocked the door and opened the store. Bishop might have wanted to be hard to read, but from the set of his jaw, Dakota could tell this wasn't just a regular visit. After a three-day absence, had she been replaced already?

"I was hoping to talk to you before your staff arrived." He set the box on the counter and clasped his hands.

She pulled off her coat and hung it over her arm and tried to delay his announcement. "You have drawings to show me?"

He stepped closer. "Why didn't you answer your phone last night?"

"My sister is in town. I've been going non-stop since her plane landed. Would you like to have a shift being her personal servant?"

"So, you had something legitimate to do?" His shoulders seemed to relax.

"I shouldn't have to explain my behavior, but yes," she said. "I thought you were here for something more serious."

"I wasn't asking you to explain. I'm just trying to understand what's going on. What did you think I was going to say?" He held her by her shoulders. She couldn't pull away.

"I don't know. Forget I said anything."

"No." He lifted her chin. "What? Dakota, say what you were really thinking."

She shrugged her shoulders hoping to mask her embarrassment. "Okay. I thought you were coming to break up with me. There, I said it. Are you happy now?"

"Hell no, I'm not happy. Why would you think that?" He released her and rubbed his forehead. His eyes were dark and intense and he wouldn't break contact.

"We had several weeks of fun. Now you might be ready to get back to your reality. You in your world and me in mine."

His face went blank.

"You have paperwork I need to review?" she asked.

"Don't do that, Dakota. Don't brush me off like what we have is insignificant. I came to see you. I wanted to see you."

He placed his hands palm down on the counter, his eyes riveted on her as if he dared her to believe him.

She bit her lower lip and nodded. For several moments, he stared at her, not moving and barely breathing. All she wanted was standing before her, but she was afraid to claim him. He wasn't the type of man who lived in a white house with a picket fence and 2.4 children. He couldn't be tamed, no matter how much love she bestowed on him.

"I need your signature here, here, and here." He pointed to separate lines on the paper and then handed her a pen, removing the cap with a loud click.

Dakota complied, scribbling her name with a flourish. "Does the work start today?"

"The crew should arrive at noon. You'll only have use of half of the store at a time. I'll help you move the books."

"You're doing manual labor?" She chuckled. The tension between them disappeared like salt in water.

"Sure. Why is that so funny?" He pulled up his sleeves, exposing his muscular forearms.

"What is this going to cost me?"

"Dinner tonight." He didn't hesitate.

She folded her arms over her chest. "Dinner?"

"Yeah, the last meal of the day. I'm sure you've eaten dinner before."

She bit her lip. "Bishop, I enjoy your company."

"Enjoy?" He nudged her shoulder with his.

"Okay, I really have a good time with you. A swinging-from the-chandelier good time. But I think I'm rebounding. It had been a while since I…since…you know—"

He grabbed her hand and ran his thumb over her palm. "What are we arguing about? You're having a good time. I'm having a good time. Usually that means keep doing what you're doing. When the good times stops being fun, then run in the opposite direction."

"You could talk a woman out of her designer shoes."

"Let's start right now." He placed his mouth over hers. His lips were warm and wet. He pulled away before she did. "I could do this all day, but we really need to move some books, or your store will be chaotic for longer than you can imagine."

She opened the lid on the box of donuts and selected a glazed one. After taking a bite, she held it up to his lips.

"You'll need your stamina," she said.

He took a huge bite and licked his lips. "I like the sound of that. Your place or mine?" He kissed her on the neck, making a circle on her flesh with his tongue.

"Books, Bishop. Books." She pointed to the far side of the store.

They worked through the morning together in silence. She motioned, he followed. The pile of books disappeared slowly.

As she made her way across the room, Bishop grabbed her by the waist. "You know this is fun. I could do this all day."

"If you keep stopping to kiss me, we will be here all day. We'll still be doing this when the contractors come to take down the walls."

She wasn't just having fun. This was serious. When he wasn't with her, she was thinking about seeing him. When he was there, she didn't want to let him go. Her grandmother always said a soft head made for a broken heart.

"Well, if you didn't wear those tight jeans and those tiny tops that barely cover your tits, I would concentrate. Do you even own a pair of sweatpants?"

She giggled. "The next time I'm at your place, I'll grab a pair of yours."

"Deal." He pinned her against the wall and kissed her. "How about tonight?"

She lifted her eyebrow. "My sister is here and she's a handful. Your mother will be here tomorrow. Anything we might want to do will have to wait."

"I don't care. I want to see you."

"Maybe I'll drive up after Melissa goes to bed.

"Maybe I'll stay at your house." He nuzzled her neck.

"Believe me, you don't want to be there while Melissa is in town. If I could escape, I would." She pushed her index finger into his chest.

"I'll be glad when our relatives go back to their respective places so you and I can get back to our lives."

There it was again. The carrot dangling in front of her nose that hinted they just might have a future together. As much as she knew she should ignore the suggestion that he was only talking, her imagination was already running away with the idea.

§§§

Dakota sat in the middle of the empty bookstore and rubbed her knees. Surrounded by a layer of dust and tools, she was exhausted. The last contractor waved goodbye and closed the door on his way out.

She had an hour before she needed to pick up Melissa and head to dinner at Asa's house. Finding the energy to get up off the floor took five minutes of her precious life.

Once she got moving, she gathered her things, locked the door and hurried to her car. She rushed into the house, kicking off her shoes on her way to the shower. They were going to be late for dinner. Dakota ran around in a frenzy getting ready. Finally dressed and hopping on one foot as she slipped on her heels, she yelled for her sister to head outside. Melissa got in the car.

"Why is the weather always so miserable here? Every time I come the temperature is below freezing."

Dakota kissed her sister's cheek. "It's not freezing. The temperature is forty degrees. Stick around for a few more weeks and you'll see real cold." Now Dakota knew how Bishop felt when she was always complaining about the temperature. She took the exit ramp to Pennsylvania Avenue.

"Now I remember why I moved to California. I think my toes are frostbitten." She leaned forward and looked at her feet.

"You knew better than to wear sandals in October in Bristol. How could you forget that?"

"I left California in a hurry. I wasn't thinking." She crossed her arms and stared at Dakota. "You know, if you had a cell phone I could have called you and asked you to buy me a pair of boots. Why don't you have one yet? Before I leave, you will have the latest cell phone."

"Melissa, you're going to have to take it down a notch or two. I don't operate in high gear, like you. I don't need a cell phone. And why didn't you just get a pair of boots out of my closet?"

"Everything in your closet is neon yellow. I want something a little more sedate."

Between the renovation, Bishop, and now Melissa, Dakota felt like she was being squeezed out of her own life. Getting the store redone was supposed to be her highest priority, but she'd been so busy having fun with Bishop, the store was the last thing she thought about. Now with Melissa crammed in her spare bedroom, she was struggling to stay focused on anything.

"Are you going to tell me what's got you wound even tighter than usual?" Dakota asked.

"I know. I'm a grouch. That's why Darius is having an affair."

Dakota stole a quick glance at her sister. "Are you serious? He wouldn't."

"If he's not, he's found something way more exciting to do almost every night of the week and someone else to do it with." Melissa rubbed her right wrist.

"You know you have a habit of exaggerating things. Are you sure you're not doing that now?"

"I'm sure. That's why I'm here. I may consider moving back."

"Oh, Melissa. Don't say that. You're crazy about Darius. Don't you think you need to confirm your accusations before you decide to leave him?"

"I didn't come here for advice. I'm just going to enjoy my time with my sisters."

Dakota took a long breath. She loved her sister, but life was complicated enough without throwing Melissa's crap in the middle of everything else going on.

"Fair enough, Melissa. We can commiserate together. As long as you let me go first each day."

They rode in silence until they pulled in front of Asa's house.

"Asa told me you're dating." Melissa grabbed her bag from the backseat and followed Dakota.

"I wouldn't say I'm 'dating'. We're just hanging out until something else comes along."

Melissa nodded with her nose in the air. "That could work, if you like sexually transmitted diseases."

"I'm not stupid, Melissa."

"I didn't mean to imply you were. I'm just...I... Forget I said that. I'm just upset with Darius. Let's change the subject. Your place looks good. You cleaned up for me."

"Yeah," But I'm sure the room doesn't meet your standards."

Melissa dropped her head. "I'm sorry. I promised I wouldn't be a pain while I'm here and so far, that's all I've been. No wonder Darius wants to leave me. I grab hold of something and I can't let go." She climbed the stairs. "I'll be a better houseguest. You won't even know I'm there."

"I doubt that." Dakota dropped her head and spoke into her scarf.

§§§

Dakota looked around the dinner table at her sisters. The three of them hadn't been together since Asa's show at Fashion Week in September Guilt tugged at her heart when she glanced at her watch. She should have been enjoying the short time they had together, but thoughts of Bishop kept popping into her head.

"So how is married life and motherhood? Is it everything you thought it would be?" Melissa asked Asa.

"Awesome. But you know that. I'm always talking about Simeon or the baby. So what are you and Darius doing? Have you two found a way to be married in the limelight?" Asa beamed while slicing a piece of salmon with her fork and taking a bite.

Melissa shook her head. "I don't know. Right now Darius is doing his thing and I'm trying to do mine. While I'm here, let's not talk about him. I'd rather talk about Dakota and her boy toy." Melissa picked up her glass of wine without taking a sip.

"Bishop is not my boy-toy."

Both sisters stared at her, as if they were waiting for her to say something profound. "I know this is going to sound ridiculous and I can't believe it myself, but I'm falling for him. I didn't mean to. And maybe I'm ridiculous, but what we have feels right."

"Oh, Dakota. You know better, honey." Melissa's voice was filled with pity.

"Melissa, you're being too harsh. You don't even know Bishop." Asa put her fork down and glared at Melissa.

"I just think she needs to slow down. Enjoy her freedom for a while."

"I've had a year of freedom and being alone while I was supposed to be in a relationship. So going slow is the last thing I want. Pleasuring myself wasn't any fun."

"Ohh, I hear you, girl." Asa gave her a high five.

Melissa readjusted her napkin in her lap and surveyed them. The disapproving smile of their older sister was familiar. She was always being the parent, taking life more serious than she should.

"Asa, I see you've gotten over Simeon tearing down the house to build the Community Center." Melissa pushed her broccoli around her plate without looking up. Asa faced her. "I only thought I wanted the family house. What I really wanted was a family of my own. Simeon's vision was a good one. The community needed that center way more than I needed that house. I have boxes of memories I can look at any time I miss Mom and Dad or Mim and Pepe. I have no complaints."

Melissa shoved her plate away. "Aren't we supposed to be talking about the community center grand opening?"

"We're all set for tomorrow. Simeon's company handled everything. I gave some ideas, but all we have to do is put on our best dresses and show up." Asa shrugged her shoulder. "We've come a long way from tearing down the family house to watching the center go up."

"Hey, guess what? Bishop is bringing his family to the opening too."

Melissa clapped. "Oh great. I get to meet the mystery man." She paused. "And his family."

"Oh no. You poor thing. How did that happen?" Asa's eyes were wide, portraying the same shock that kept zapping Dakota.

"He's trying to patch up the relationship between his parents and his sister. The opening is just a way to get them together." Dakota tried to keep her voice even. There was no need to let her sisters know the thought of meeting his parents had her panicked.

"Leave it to Dakota to bring the drama." Melissa raised her glass in the air before taking a sip.

"There won't be any drama. I'll be on my best behavior."

"And we will look like a million dollars, because I've designed a gown for each of us."

Melissa and Dakota squealed in unison.

"No way!" Melissa smacked the table.

"Yes, I did. We'll be in the same color, but different styles."

Tears ran down Melissa's cheeks. She grabbed the napkin and wiped her face. For the tough one, she sure cried easy

"Okay, you two, that's enough. We're supposed to be celebrating. We sacrificed Mim and Pepe's house in order to have the community center." Asa reached for her sister's hands and squeezed. "So, no matter what happens tomorrow, it's going to be fun."

Chapter Twenty

Bishop turned off the phone and shoved it into his breast pocket. The feel of the black organic wool, Gucci tuxedo was the only comfort he'd had all day. Handling his parents and sister frayed his patience. Since his parents' plane had landed, his mother had acquired a permanent frown that grew bigger every time Adana's husband Dennis spoke to her.

Sooner or later, Adanna needed to stand up and be her own woman. If Mom and Dad didn't like what she had to say, she'd just have to accept their response and move on.

He jumped in the car. With a big sigh, he started the engine. With all the careful planning, tonight should go just fine. At least his mother was speaking to Adanna, even if the two of them had fallen back into their pattern of poking fun at him.

Now if everyone's good mood could last through the Community Center Opening Gala, then he'd count this as a good evening. But introducing Dakota, his treasure, to his family would be the highlight of the evening.

He grinned. For the first time in his life, the need for his father's approval was non-existent. There was nothing shameful about loving one woman and wanting to please her. His father might have been too foolish to realize how important the right woman could be, but Bishop wanted to hold on to Dakota with both hands and make sure she knew how he felt.

The extra one hundred dollars he'd slipped the driver should ensure his family arrived at the celebration about ten minutes before he showed up with Dakota. He changed lanes and took the Route 273 exit.

A parking space in front of Dakota's stylish townhouse made parking easy. He turned off the car and hopped out. After ringing the bell, he adjusted his bow tie.

She opened the door. The hot pink, off-the-shoulder gown hugged her hips and butt. The deep V-neck neckline exposed the beautiful mounds of her breasts. He wanted to slip his hand under the delicate fabric and squeeze them. "You look amazing, sweetie." He pressed his lips to her cheek.

"What? I can't get any tongue action tonight?" She smiled up at him.

"I don't want to muss your glossy lips. But I'm putting in a reservation for extra lips tonight, with all the trimmings."

"You mean I'm going to have to wait all night for a kiss? That doesn't seem fair."

"No. I have to wait all night to taste you and to see what's under that lovely dress, so believe me, I'm the one who's really suffering."

She grabbed her purse and tucked it under her arm. "We better go. I don't want to be late."

As soon as they pulled away, she faced him. "How's the visit with your parents going? Have Adanna and your mother patched up their relationship?"

"They're doing well, so far." He kept his eyes on the road. "But neither Mom nor Dad have said more than ten words to Dennis. He doesn't know how lucky he is. But they love DJ."

"Do you think she'll come around?" Dakota's stomach cramped. His parents' approval was important to the him. What would they think of her?

"Let's see, after he defiled my baby sister, I think it will take more than one visit to mend that fence. Mom is a tough bird."

Dakota folded her hands in her lap. "I see."

"She's not that bad. You've met Dennis, so you know he's a hard person to take a liking to."

"He's trying, and his love for Adana and DJ is obvious. Isn't that the most important thing of all?"

"Not by a long shot." He pulled the car under the extended portico. A valet opened the passenger and driver doors.

With his hand around Dakota's waist, he escorted her inside. Instead of her fluid gait, she seemed stiff.

"You're not worried about meeting my parents, are you?"

"Yes. I'm scared to death."

"I won't let them eat you for dinner." He laughed.

§§§

Dakota pasted a smile on her face. Tonight wasn't supposed to be about meeting Bishop's parents. After all the turmoil that almost tore Simeon and Asa apart while they fought over the Conroy family house, tonight should be a jubilant celebration. Instead, she couldn't think of anything but meeting Bishop's mother and father.

A hint of resentment simmered in her belly. His parents changed the flavor of the whole night As long as she and Bishop stayed in their cocoon, life was great. Intrusions from the outside world could shake everything loose. The critical glare of his parents' eyes could be enough for Bishop to see her flaws and insecurities.

She tilted her chin a little higher. No matter what, she was going to have a good time. Even though she felt like someone had run a stick up the back of her dress, making it impossible to walk.

Asa and Simeon stood hand in hand at the entrance, greeting the guests as they arrived. One day, she'd find someone special. Brian wasn't The One. Bishop didn't want to be The One. But that didn't mean she'd stop looking for The One. The only question she needed to address was how long she planned to play this game. Pretty soon, she needed to step off this merry go-round and get back in the real world.

"Dakota, you look fabulous. That dress fits you perfectly. I'll have to make sure the photographer gets a picture of you for the website." Asa embraced her, but not tight enough to wrinkle the dress.

"You look pretty fantastic yourself." Dakota eyed her sister from head to foot. "And look at you, Simeon, still as handsome as ever."

"All I can say is that every Conroy sister looks incredible tonight." Simeon brushed his lips across her cheek. "Your table is near the podium. Bishop, your family is already seated." Simeon pointed to the far corner.

"Where is Melissa sitting?" Dakota asked.

"She's at our table, nursing a drink. Her second one tonight. Maybe you can cheer her up," Asa said. "And don't roll your eyes at me. I saw that."

Bishop grabbed Dakota's hand. "We might as well get the hard part over. You've met Adanna and Dennis. Let's meet my Mom and Dad."

Dakota tightened her grip on his hand as he led her across the hardwood floor. She waved at familiar faces. Several of the residents who had sold their home in the old Golden Leaf neighborhood to make way for the center were seated near the stage.

"That you, Dakota?" Ms. Donald called to her from her table.

"Ms. Donald, don't you look pretty tonight?" Dakota greeted the older woman.

"I should, child. This dress cost me a year's worth of books."

"Don't worry about it, your credit is good with me. I'd like for you to meet my date, Bishop Contee."

"Pleased to meet you, young man." She shook his hand before returning her attention to the woman seated next to her.

"Date? Is that what I am to you, just a date?"

She pulled back to glare at him. "What should I have said? What's wrong with the word date? I'm nervous enough about meeting your parents, please don't..."

His faced hardened. "Nothing. It's fine."

Dakota spotted a man seated across the room. The regal set of his jaw coupled with his dashing good looks could only belong to Bishop's father. His attention was focused on the backside of a woman at the next table. It was evident which tree Bishop branched from.

His mother held her arms tight across her abdomen. The smile on her face looked about as fake as the one that Dakota tried to wear. If she stayed with Bishop, would that be her ten years from now?

"Mom, Dad, I want you to meet Dakota. A very good friend of mine." Bishop gave her a knowing look. She'd remember his introduction for future use.

Dakota almost curtsied. The tension around the table was almost visible.

"I'm happy to meet you, dear." Ms. Contee stuck out her hand for Dakota to shake. "Call me Madeline, please." The nasal sound of her voice sounded rehearsed, a forced politeness.

"It's nice to meet you, Madeline."

Mr. Contee pushed away from the table and opened his arms. "Well, honey I'm from the old school. Give me a hug." He enveloped her in his arms before she could object.

"Sit down here so we can talk." Madeline patted the chair next to her. "Bishop, why don't you and Dennis get us a glass of wine? Please."

"I need to stretch my legs, too." Mr. Contee pushed away from the table and trailed behind Bishop out of the room. Even though he had to be nearing sixty, he was still a good-looking man. Madeline's lips tightened into a scowl as her husband hurried toward the door.

Dakota took the seat and watched Bishop disappear in the crowd, leaving her in the lion's den.

"Tell me about yourself. Dakota, is it?" Madeline lifted her nose another inch.

"Let's see." Dakota folded her hands on the table. "I own a small local bookstore here in Bristol. I'm a graduate of Morgan State University in Baltimore, Liberal Arts."

"You're quite an accomplished woman. That's quite refreshing. So, Bishop told me your family donated the land for this community center. That's quite commendable."

"We didn't donate all the land. Several residents gave up their homes. And we all were paid handsomely on the deal." Dakota glanced down, unable to meet Madeline's stare. Instead of chatting, this was more of an interview.

She broke into laughter. "Even better. Capitalism is alive and well." Her smile was warm. Dakota released the tension in her shoulders.

"I guess you could say that. I'm glad you and your husband were able to come help us celebrate the opening."

"Bishop was quite adamant that we had to come. I think he had other motives." She lifted a brow. "So, you and Bishop are in a relationship?"

Dakota opened her mouth to respond.

"Mom, don't you think that's a little personal? You're interrogating Dakota." A look of horror flared in Adanna's eyes.

"I'm just trying to get to know her. I'm only in town for a short time, so I have to catch up on everything. It's not like you two will call me and keep me informed."

"We call you all the time—"

"It's okay, Adanna. I don't mind."

"It's embarrassing." Adanna huffed and dropped her elbow on the table.

"They should start serving dinner soon." Dakota turned in her chair to look for Bishop.

"How long have you known Bishop?" Madeline continued.

"Several weeks."

Bishop and Dennis returned just as dinner was being served.

"Where's your father?" Madeline craned her neck to look at the entrance.

"He's coming." Bishop placed a glass of wine in front of her before taking his seat.

"Yeah, I'm sure he is." Madeline's sarcasm dripped on the table like hot wax.

Sandwiched between Bishop and his mother made dinner seem long and intense. His mother's "interrogation" continued through the first three courses. She peppered Dakota with questions as if she was on a fact-finding mission, trying to determine if Dakota was good enough for her son. By the time dessert was served, Dakota was exhausted.

"Honey, I'll be right back. I want to take a look around at the facility." Mr. Contee dashed away from the table before Madeline could open her mouth.

"Dakota, I'd like to have lunch with you before I leave. Do you think that's possible?"

She looked at Bishop before responding, hoping he'd give her a way out. Instead, he gave her a big smile.

"Sure, Madeline. I'd like that." Dakota's stomach constricted. "Can you all excuse me for a moment? I need to go to the ladies' room." Without waiting for anyone to reply, she jumped up from the table.

"Walk with me," she whispered in Asa's ear as she rushed by their table.

In the restroom, she leaned against the cool tile wall with her hands on her hips. Asa and Melissa rushed in behind her.

"What's wrong? Are you sick?" Melissa placed her hand on Dakota's forehead.

"No, but I'm sick of Bishop's mother. She has asked me nine hundred questions since I got here. Any minute now, she's going to ask me for a blood and urine sample. I know it."

"Oh, honey. I'm so sorry. But you can't hide out in the bathroom." Melissa eyes were full of concern.

"She can if she wants to. Or you can come sit at our table," Asa offered.

Dakota pushed off the wall and turned on the faucet. She ran her wrists under the cold water and her breathing returned to normal.

"Why would he want me to meet his parents anyway? Doesn't that usually come months later in a relationship? Why did he invite them here?" Dakota dried her hands.

"Look, Simeon will be making his speech in a few minutes. I need to get back inside, unless you really need me, Dakota," Asa said.

"No. You go. I'll be all right."

Asa gave her another look before leaving.

Melissa rubbed her back. "Are you returning to the table?"

"Yeah. I'm okay. Let's go."

Several people were gathered in the main entrance. Dakota and her sister had to push their way through the thick crowd. Outside in the frigid night air, a few men and women took quick puffs from their cigarettes. At least they were obeying the no smoking policy. Dakota spotted Mr. Contee with his hand around the waist of a woman in a dress so short her butt had to be freezing. He took a long drag and blew smoke out the corner of his mouth.

She couldn't take her eyes off the way his hand slipped down to grasp a handful of ass and the open-mouthed kiss the woman gave him. With his wife just a few feet away, how could he behave so brazen? Is that what happened when playboys aged?

"What are you looking at?" Melissa asked.

"Nothing. Let's go."

Chapter Twenty-One

Dakota sat outside the restaurant, checking the rearview mirror. Madeline was already inside. She could see her seated at the table near the window. After last night, Dakota had more respect for Madeline. It took a tough woman to hold her family together when her husband was doing everything he could to tear it apart. The idea of monogamy was great in theory, but it seemed a lot harder to put into practice. Even her parents had died with the suspicion of infidelity in the air.

She shook the thought away. Dating Bishop was playing with fire. But while she thought she was having fun, he'd claimed her heart. He wasn't any closer to giving up his playboy ways than she was of enduring their casual relationship.

She stepped out of the car and headed inside.

Madeline waved to her as she came through the door.

"I was beginning to wonder if you were going to show." Madeline slid her chair to the left to make room at the small table. The morning paper lay open in front of her.

"I'm sorry to keep you waiting. I couldn't get away from the bookstore. Jennifer was late this morning. Have you ordered yet?" Dakota picked up the menu.

"Of course not. I was waiting for you. I see the little affair last night made the front page. I think that's very quaint. In La Jolla, something this small wouldn't have been a blip on the screen of activity. I find it rather surprising that Bishop could be happy in such a small city." She held her nose in the air like a bad smell had entered the room.

"Madeline, Bishop doesn't live in Bristol. And Philadelphia is no hick city. I think Philly can compete with any cosmopolitan city."

"Yes, of course. I didn't mean to belittle the town or the affair. Everything was quite charming."

The server arrived to take their orders, then disappeared. "I had hoped I'd get to your bookstore while I was here. I'd like to see your establishment."

"You haven't missed much. It's under renovation. I'll make sure to send you pictures of the finished project."

She placed the napkin in her lap. "Dakota, I'm nothing if I'm not straightforward. After

Adanna's little debacle, I decided my hands-off approach is probably not the best idea."

"Madeline, if you have something on your mind, just say it."

She patted Dakota hands. "I thought so, dear. You seem to be quite reasonable. Level headed. You run a successful business. But honey, don't fall in love with my son. You'll end up hurt and bitter. Bishop can't help himself. A gene passed on from his father, or after being raised by his father, he doesn't stand a chance. In this case the apple doesn't fall from the tree."

Dakota opened her mouth to respond, but hesitated. How could she answer his mother when she had so many questions herself? "We've only been dating a short time. I'm not sure how I'd classify our relationship, but I think we are a long way from serious." She shrugged.

"Oh, dear." She looked distressed.

"Does he know we're having this conversation?"

"Of course not. I just wish someone had told me what I was getting into when I fell head-over-heels for his father. He doesn't think I see what's going on. But every new piece of jewelry that he brought home meant he'd slept with another bimbo."

Dakota pictured Bishop's father as he groped the buttocks of the woman half his age last night. "Why do you put up with his behavior?"

"I used to think about leaving him, but when I turned fifty, I realized I didn't want to start a new life. I have a nice home, with a clothes and shoe closet that would make other women drool. I take several wonderful trips each year and I have a core of girlfriends that are wonderful. When I need to complain, they listen. I've decided I'm too old to change my life now. But if I'd known in my twenties or thirties that he was going to be this kind of man, I would have taken my babies and run in the opposite direction."

Madeline picked up her water glass and took a sip. The diamond on her ring finger could choke an elephant. After she put the glass down, she stacked her hands on the table. "I'm not proud to admit this, but…" She looked across the room. "It's financial. I like the nice vacations, the designer clothes, and the big house. And I'm not walking away with only half."

"Why are you telling me this? You hardly know me."

"I see the way you look at him." She picked up her glass again. "You love him. And Bishop might think he's falling for you. I think that's why he insisted we come to town. He wanted to show you off. But your relationship is still shiny and new. I'm not so sure he can hold on to that kind of passion for thirty or forty years."

A thin film of sweat moistened Dakota's back. She knew what she was getting into, to say anything less than that wouldn't be fair to Bishop. But his mother's sharp words pierced her heart like a blade.

"Ms. Contee…Madeline. Bishop has always been honest with me. We have a no-strings relationship. I'm not sure what you think you know about me, but I'm a big girl. I can take care of myself."

Madeline made a loud sucking sound with her teeth and shook her head. "If I thought Bishop or his brothers were capable of change, I wouldn't be sitting here. I'm surprised he didn't warn you. Out of all of my boys, he is usually the most honest one."

Dakota sat back in her chair. She pressed her hand together in her lap to keep from fondling some miscellaneous item on the table. "One of the first things Bishop told me about himself was that he's not into commitment."

"You think you can change him?"

"No. I'm not ready to settle down, either. So our relationship works for us."

"Let me tell you something about Contee men. Keep your heart tucked away. Someone should have stopped Adanna before she got carried away with Dennis. He's not much better."

"You don't believe in marriage?"

She fingered the edge of the napkin. "Senior is slowing down now. Most nights I know exactly where he is. I'm not saying he isn't a good man. He just wasn't good husband material when he was young. He's taking a long time to grow up. But after all these years of marriage, I don't much care what he does anymore. He lives his life and I live mine. And I must say, I always manage to find good company when I'm in need."

The server returned with lunch. Dakota looked at the large green apple salad and swallowed. No way could she sit through a meal.

"Darling, you look sick. Are you feeling well?" Madeline reached for her hand.

"If you could excuse me, I need to go to the ladies' room." Dakota pushed away from the table and grabbed her purse.

In the lounge, she sat on the sofa and buried her head in her palms. Her stomach churned like a cake mixer. She deserved exactly what she got. Mim used to say, if you play with fire, don't cry when you get burned.

"Ma'am, are you okay? Can I get you something?"

Dakota looked up to find a server hunched over her with a paper towel in her hand. "I'm fine. Thank you." Dakota stood and smoothed the wrinkles from her dress. After a deep breath, she slogged back to the dining room.

Chapter Twenty-Two

After lunch Dakota kissed Madeline's cheek and waved goodbye. She was happy to see Madeline tip off in her five-inch heels to the rented Jaguar and pull away.

When she was out of sight, Dakota started the Volkswagen and headed for the bookstore. At least during the remainder of their lunch Madeline hadn't revealed any more family secrets that Dakota would rather not know about.

Sorting out Bishop's mother's words from all the emotions was like trying to find that infamous missing sock, impossible. All she wanted to do was erase the thought that she could become Madeline. Even though Madeline was a beautiful, fashionable woman, the sadness in her words was a warning.

The time she'd spent with Bishop didn't match his confession about wanting to be unattached. He showed up even when she wasn't expecting him, he called several times a day, and he always made her feel special. Brian had never been that attentive and he'd never confessed he didn't want attachment. What could she believe? Was it all part of Bishop's charm, or did it really mean something.

People changed. Maybe he was ready for a real relationship, or maybe she just wanted him to be.

The balance of the day, she maneuvered customers around the construction as they made book selections. The banging of hammers and the constant chatter cushioned her through the day.

For the first time in years, she was happy to lock the doors of the shop and head home. Only in the sanctuary of her small home did she stop guarding her emotions. Before Bishop arrived, she dimmed the lights and folded her legs into the lotus position on the floor. No way could she feel bad about how they ended up. She got just what she told him she wanted, fun and excitement. Together, they had both.

After several minutes, she opened a bottle of wine and lit some candles. The doorbell interrupted the peacefulness. Before answering, she checked the mirror and fluffed her hair, hating herself for even caring about such small things.

"When did you become that person?" she asked her reflection before turning away.

Bishop stood on the threshold with a big smile and a bouquet of long-stemmed yellow roses. "I owe you a thousand thank yous for putting up with my family over the weekend. I put my parents on a plane this evening, and now I'm all yours again." He slipped his hand behind her neck and drew her close enough to kiss. His cold hands sent a shiver through her.

The moment she tasted his tongue, she realized how much she'd missed him if she sent him on his way, or if he decided to move on. When his family gene rang the bell, signaling her time was up and the next lucky woman could take his hand in his long line of female companionship, she'd be left alone and lonely.

"Flowers? That's a first. Should I consider myself special or do you do this for all your girlfriends?" She led him into the kitchen.

"I'm not a flower giver, so this is special. You are special. After the weekend you've had to put up with, I figured I should do something to thank you."

"I had an interesting conversation with your mother today at lunch."

"Any conversation with my outspoken mother can be interesting. So what did dear old Mom say this time?" He poured the wine.

"She talked about the family gene that makes the Contee men unable to settle down like it was a real scientific phenomenon."

He took a long swallow. "She likes telling that story. Telling her side make her feel less like a victim and more like a martyr for putting up with my dad. What else did she say?"

Dakota expected him to deny his mother's logic or to distance himself from his mother's story. Her body temperature edged up like a warning signal.

"So, what she said was true?" Mim used to say never ask a question if you don't really want the answer. She steadied herself against the counter, hoping his reply would strike his mother's belief out of existence.

"Nothing's been verified," he chuckled. "I think we kinda like the legend. But the tale has more to do with watching my father as we grew up than anything else. Adanna is the only one that's chosen the marriage route. And right now, it doesn't look like that was too wise."

"Dennis just doesn't have a lot of money. He's not mean or cruel and his feelings for his family are obvious. He adores your sister. Why don't you guys like him?"

"She could have done better, that's all."

"Love has no regard for class, Bishop." There was more edge in her voice than she wanted.

"Yeah, I know."

"What are you saying?" Dakota put her glass down to focus on him.

"What do you mean? We're just discussing your lunch with my mother, right?"

She nodded. "So, you just let the gene theory rule the way you live your life?"

"That's pretty tough. But after thirty-three years of living this life, I've lowered my expectations."

She smacked his arm. "What does that mean? While dating me, you've been slumming?" She narrowed her eyes, demanding honesty from him.

"No, you're absolutely great. I just think I'm too young to settle down forever."

"Why, is there some young ass out there that you need to grab?"

"Where did that come from?" He wrapped his arm around her and kissed her forehead.

"Never mind." She gulped her wine.

§§§

Bishop recognized the conversation the moment she started. Careful not to reveal too much, he held his gaze steady. His voice even. The last thing his father had said today before going through security was "Be careful son. That woman wants more than a good toss in the bed."

Bishop had slapped his father on the back and laughed, but he already knew Dakota wasn't the type of woman to hang around for fun, forever. He wanted more too. But just not right now. Regardless of how much he enjoyed her company, he wasn't ready to walk down the aisle.

He grabbed her hand and led her to the sofa. Ready to change the subject. "I had a hard day.

After removing his shoes, he sat beside her on the sofa. She coaxed his head into her lap.

"How's the renovation coming along? Did the shelves arrive today?" He tilted his head just enough to see her face.

With her warm fingers, she messaged his temples, loosening the tension from the day. He closed his eyes as she ran her thumbs over his forehead. Just her touch slowed down time.

"Everything is on schedule. I think we'll be done in time for small business Saturday. I run a whole ad for that day."

He chuckled. "Do you have a letter to read to me tonight?"

"I thought you didn't like my readings."

He lifted his head, pulling up next to her. He held her face between his palms to stare into her beautiful brown eyes. "I enjoy your readings."

"Are you making fun of me?"

"A little, but in a loving way."

"You better be careful or when dinner arrives, you only get to watch me eat."

"Read me something, girl." He slid his hand between the cushion and her butt.

She reached for the book on the coffee table, and flipped through several pages before landing on one. "*I will cover you with love when next I see you, with caresses, with ecstasy. I want to gorge you with all the joys of the flesh, so that you faint and die. I want you to be amazed by me and to confess to yourself that you had never even dreamed of such transports... When you are old, I want you to recall those few hours, I want your dry bones to quiver with joy when you think of them.'"*

He nodded. "I like that. Who wrote it?"

"Gustave Flaubert in 1846."

"Wow, I guess even back then men were lustful."

"Loving." She corrected him.

"You are a beautiful woman, do you know that?"

"Yeah, yeah. You're too late to clean it up now." She flipped on the music channel.

Like the music, Dakota had infiltrated his life too. This couldn't be too much different from commitment. He held her in the fold of his arm. In the serenity of her living room, his conflicted thoughts eased enough to allow him to enjoy her.

"You know we can't go on like this much longer." Her voice was so calm he almost didn't recognize the sound.

He shifted her away. "What are you talking about? That stuff my mother said?"

"She was right. Your mother. We've been having a really good time together, but we can't have a meaningless affair forever. At some point, we have to return to adult life and do adult things."

He pulled his hand down his face and glared at her. "All relationships always come to this, you know. We're having a good time and women always want to shake things up. I don't understand why. What do you want, Dakota?" He stood up, kicked the table with a big thump.

She clasped her fingers without looking up at him. "I want more than you can give me."

"You know I'm not ready to settle down. I told you that."

She pushed off the sofa. "You don't have to change. I do."

"Dammit, Dakota." He walked the length of the small room like a caged animal. "Why now, why tonight?"

"Bishop, I can wait till next month or next year, but why? If I've learned nothing else, I know I'm not putting my life on hold for another man."

"So this is about Brian again. Because of him, you're judging me," he huffed. "That fucking man is always lurking around some corner."

"That's not true. This has nothing to do with Brian. I'm talking about you and me. We are fine as long as we don't talk about the future or I don't get too serious. But I can't promise that I won't get too wrapped up in this…this thing we do."

He pushed his hands in his pockets. "So now what?" His words hung between them, like a smoldering flame nobody wanted to touch. He didn't know how to answer.

"I can't hold you with one hand and have a normal life with the other. I could wait around hoping you'd change, but Mim always said you can lead a horse to water but you can't make him drink."

"Are you sure this is what you want?"

She bit her lip.

Before she could answer, he grabbed his suit jacket off the chair and stormed out the door. He slammed it hard enough to shatter the quiet on the deserted street.

Chapter Twenty-Three

Bishop turned on the computer. He tapped his fingers on the desk while waiting for it to boot up. Until a few weeks ago, feelings and emotions seldom captured his attention for more than a moment. They changed so frequently it didn't seem necessary to get familiar with them. Then Dakota breezed into Simeon's suite and everything changed.

Baby steps were in order. She wanted to take leaps and bounds. There was no way he was ready to walk down the aisle or commit to forever. The possibility made him uneasy.

"How's it going, Bishop?"

He looked up to see Simeon in the door way. "Hey, man. Come on in and have a seat. I haven't talked with you in a while. There's lot of stuff I need to catch you up on." Bishop pointed to the chair

Simeon folded his frame in the straight chair and placed his foot on his knee. "I've been busy. I hope you don't think I've abandoned you."

"Not at all. Was Asa pleased with the setup in New York?"

"Very much. The show was all she could talk about when she got home. Thanks for handling that." An easy smile settled on Simeon's face.

"You know, I've been meaning to talk to you about Dakota. She's been through a lot this last year. She really is like a sister to me." He cleared his throat. "I know how you enjoy your… women, but just make sure you don't hurt her."

"I know she's pretty special. But you don't need to worry. She broke up with me a few days ago." He paused. "Tell me something, Simeon. How did you know when you were ready to settle down? That Asa was the one?"

Simeon's face lit up. "I knew Asa was the one in high school. I just had a lot of baggage I needed to deal with. Sometimes I still shake my head when I think how close I came to losing her. I can't imagine my life without her and Mia."

"You make marriage sound so simple. So easy."

"Our relationship wasn't hard at all when I stopped being selfish." Simeon pushed out of the seat. "Thankfully, my brother helped me see what I couldn't." He nodded and walked out.

Bishop sat in silence for several moments. Nothing in life was ever that simple. What if Dakota wasn't the one? His father had thought his mother was the right one at some point. But after a few years, when the newness wore off, he realized he hadn't made the right choice. Now he spends every day chasing something he can't catch.

His cell phone rang. Adanna's name flashed on the screen.

"What's up, sis? "

"Are you and Dakota still coming tonight?"

"Oh, Adanna. I forgot. I don't think—"

"Don't you dare say you aren't coming. Tonight's our anniversary and you promised to celebrate with us."

"The thing is, Dakota and I…well, we aren't together anymore. We haven't seen each other in several days. I'd make lousy company. How about we get together another day?"

"My anniversary is today. You see, that's how the celebration works. That's why the dinner is tonight. Bishop, you do know that sometimes the world doesn't revolve around you or your wants."

He squeezed the phone without responding.

"What happened? What stupid-ass thing did you do this time? Don't you know when you have a good thing? Do you plan to spend the rest of your life chasing pussy?"

"Why don't you tell me what you really think?" His voice was curt.

"Look, I want you here tonight at seven. The only thing that can stop you is hell and high water. Be here." She hung up the receiver.

He turned off the phone. Only sisters got to speak that way.

Simeon stuck his head in the office. "Bishop, are you free? I need you to take a ride with me. I want your opinion on a job site."

Bishop stood up. "I'd love to get out of dinner with my sister tonight, but if I don't show up, I'll be drummed out of the brother's club."

"I understand. I've been there. Good luck." Simeon headed to the elevator.

He had less than an hour to get to Adanna's, but instead of following Simeon out of the building, he fell back in his chair. It was just easier to ignore everything. Tonight Adanna would want to know what happened and he had no answers. If he did, he could have fixed things months or years ago when the example he was shown was faulty.

Bishop packed up the computer and left the office. As he pulled out of the parking garage, he turned toward Bristol.

A block from Dakota's house. He smacked the steering wheel. "Dammit!"

No way would he beg her to change her mind. He jerked the steering wheel to get in the right lane and away from her house. He wouldn't get to dinner on time. He drove up Kirkwood Highway without turning on his radio.

"You're fifteen minutes late and why aren't you answering your phone? I've been calling you." Adanna greeted him at her front door.

"I had some business to take care of at work. Besides I needed some quiet time." He hugged his sister.

"Dinner is ready, so wash your hands and come on." She returned to the kitchen.

He did as requested before returning to the dining room.

"Dennis, how do you put up with that mouth? She's so bossy." He sat down at the table.

"Just let her talk and nod." Dennis laughed.

Adanna put platters of food on the table. "I can hear you two." She sat next to DJ to feed him.

"What smells so good?" Bishop tickled DJ's chin. The round-faced baby tapped his spoon on the highchair tray.

"I cooked all of Dennis's favorites: lamb chops, sweet potato casserole, and collard greens. Now tell me what happened with Dakota. She was the best thing that ever happened to you." She pushed a spoonful of strained spinach at her son.

"Let's just say we found out we wanted different things."

"What? She wanted commitment and you wanted to continue to chase every short skirt within a ten-mile radius?"

"Aren't you going to help me out, Dennis?" He looked to his brother-in-law.

"Nope. You can handle this one."

Adanna continued to feed DJ, switching to carrots.

"I don't chase skirts. I haven't been on a date since Dakota and I stopped seeing each other."

"Why not? Don't tell me you're pinning for Dakota. How does that feel?"

He hunched his shoulders and glared at his sister. "I'm just not interested right now. I got some stuff I need to sort out. Now get out of my business, why don't you?"

"I think it's happened. The mighty Bishop Contee finally met his match."

He looked down at his plate and shoved the potatoes aside.

"Your food is getting cold. Aren't you going to eat?" Bishop asked.

"I always feed DJ first." She wiped the baby's face as he spit carrots down his chin and onto her hand.

"Here, let me feed him while you eat." He pulled DJ from the highchair and balanced him on his knee. The baby grabbed his tie, smearing a mixture of spinach and carrots into the tip.

Bishop kissed his nephew on the forehead.

§§§

In the quiet restaurant, Dakota glanced around the table at her sister Asa. Thank God she'd moved back to Bristol. Being able to share stuff lessened the load on her shoulders. Life had the possibility to be good even if there was no leading man in it right now. Even the ache in her heart had dull a little since Bishop decided his life would be easier if he walked away than to commit. It seemed like she was viewing life through a pair of dark shades in a dim room. The lackluster appearance of everything drew her energy, leaving her lethargic.

She could have continued being Bishop's girlfriend forever. But Mim's words wouldn't leave her alone. If you make yourself a doormat, don't cry when people walk on you. So she had to do something different. She didn't want to be the girlfriend in a ten-year relationship.

Dakota tried to smile and lifted her wine glass to her sister. "To us. May we always find happiness."

"I'll drink to that." Asa clicked her glass to Dakota's and took a long swallow.

Dakota reached for her hand and gave it a squeeze. "We've had a whirlwind year, haven't we? But we can always count on each other. Through the good and the bad."

"So what's up with that good-looking Bishop? I haven't seen him hanging around lately." Asa focused her attention on Dakota.

"Bishop was a fling. We had fun for a while. He didn't want anything serious and I'm not arm candy to be thrown in the back of the closet like yesterday's shoes."

Asa picked up her glass. "I heard that." She took a sip. "Two years ago I was going through some stuff with Simeon. Now this is your time and Melissa's. You'll find the right person."

"Words of wisdom from my sister." Dakota pushed her plate away. "So should we start planning Christmas activities? East coast or west coast?"

"East coast," Asa responded. "Let's celebrate the holiday at my place. I have plenty of room."

"I'm in. But I don't think you need to plan on lots of folks. Melissa may be alone and I'm certain I will be."

Asa nodded. "Let's pay the check and get out of here. I need to get home and see my baby before she goes to bed."

In the parking lot, Dakota waved to her sister. As much as she loved her, a little time alone was on the agenda. Spending Christmas in the quiet of her home held some appeal. She could buy herself something decadently expensive, a good bottle of wine, the finest hummus money could buy, and curl up with a good movie. Just the thought of smiling and trying to be happy during all the festivity was too much to think about.

She couldn't stop thinking about Bishop, wondering what he was doing and whom he was doing it with. She glanced at her watch and tried to imagine him going out with a new woman draped over his arm. Had he ever been serious about her? At least he never professed more than he was capable of giving. So many nights she came within a heartbeat of confessing her love for him. Thankfully she was saved that embarrassment.

In front of her house, she turned off the car. With her hands still on the steering wheel, she peered at the front door. Maybe she needed to get away. A trip to a sunny, warm spot with tropical drinks could put her in a better state of mind. There was no way her sisters could deny she needed a vacation.

A knock on the passenger side window startled her. She glanced over expecting to see Bishop and his big smile. Instead the large blue eyes of Sharon were drilled on her.

This woman was a kook. Dakota wondered if she should pull off and leave her standing on the sidewalk. But she refused to run away, accepting whatever life dished up her.

She swallowed, grabbed her purse, and got out of the car. Balancing the weight of the knapsack on her fingers, she was convinced the weight was heavy enough to pack a wallop if needed.

"Sharon, why are you here?" She tried to sound like an authority.

"I think you know why. Bishop…" She began to cry. "Bishop really loves me and if you step out of the way he'll realize his feelings for me."

"This has nothing to do with me." Dakota took a step back.

"It has everything to do with you. He thinks you're special." She wiped her nose with her hand.

"I think this is a conversation you need to have with him. Stalking me isn't the answer."

"You need to tell him…tell him." She raised her hand and Dakota backed up another inch.

If only life were that simple. Dakota pulled the strap of her purse onto her shoulder. "Sharon, Bishop doesn't belong to me. He makes his own decisions."

"He won't take my calls. He won't see me." Sharon's declaration sounded pitiful. Mascara ran down her face, leaving a dark trail on her cheek.

"To love someone who doesn't love you is one of those cruel twists life throws at our feet. Stepping over the hurt and moving on is the only thing you can control." Dakota touched Sharon's arm, hoping to comfort her. "I don't know what to tell you. But are you sure this is what you want?"

Sharon shook her head. Tears flowed in a steady stream onto her coat. "I'm sorry. I shouldn't have come here. This is wrong. I'm acting like a crazy person. This whole thing is just driving me over the edge. You must think I'm a lunatic."

"This is pretty insane." Dakota tried to smile.

Sharon drew a deep breath while looking down the street. "Okay. I'm going now. Can we pretend this never happened?"

"If you want, we can do that."

She nodded and walked away without another word. Dakota rubbed her hands together, wishing she had gloves. When Sharon disappeared around the corner, Dakota climbed the stairs.

She unlocked the door, then heard the phone ring. She rushed to the kitchen and looked at the caller ID. Bishop's number was on the display. With her hand on the receiver, she wanted to lift it to her ear and hear his smooth voice tickle her heart. Her fingers tightened around the hard plastic, but she refused to pick up.

The phone stopped ringing. Her stomach dropped like an elevator with a broken cable. Without releasing her hold on the phone, she closed her eyes until the feeling passed. Even if she didn't get the man, she got some satisfaction. She wasn't running away anymore. The phone rang again as she charged up the stairs.

Chapter Twenty-Four

The sparkle and shine of Bookends made the six weeks of destruction all worthwhile. Even if the renovation took a week longer than the original estimate the dust, dirt ,and noise was worth the aggravation. Dakota opened the dusty box of Christmas ornaments. She lifted a red tree ornament and a green one. In the new design, these old decorations wouldn't do. She needed something that said this was a hip, new place.

Jennifer walked in and tucked her coat across her am. "Is it that time already to put up a tree?" She placed her hand on her hip. "You know I don't think I'll ever get used to putting my coat in a closet. Jennifer disappeared to the back of the store, mumbling as she walked.

The door to the store opened again. Dakota looked up to see Bishop strolling toward the counter. The pen in her hand began to shake. Without taking a deep breath, she tried to fill her lungs with air. She tried to tamp down the emotions churning in her stomach. She tried to appear normal. He could have shown up in her store for any number of reasons. Probably to see the finished product of his handiwork.

"What are you doing here?"

He gave her a smile. The empty weeks vanished. She wanted to walk into his arms and live the dreams she'd envisioned. Instead, she remained by the register. The counter put the right amount of distance between them.

"I've been trying to get in touch with you."

"I've been ignoring your calls."

He rested his elbow on the counter. "Why?"

"Did you want to talk to me about the renovation? Something to do with the store?"

She wanted her voice to sound casual and light not like the voice of an angry lover, the way Sharon had sounded a few weeks ago.

His smile penetrated the shield around her heart. "No. I wanted to talk to you. We can still talk, can't we?"

She stood in front of him. "Yes, we can do that." She released the breath she'd been holding. His smile widened. "How have you been? I missed you."

She took a step. "I'm doing okay. Business has picked up, so I'm keeping me busy."

"I don't want to hear about the store. I'm asking about you. I miss you." He reached for her hand and pulled her to the edge of the counter.

Dakota gave him a half smile. "I'm pretty busy right now. Maybe we can talk later."

"This is a bookstore. I came to buy books." His heavy voice sent a wave of nostalgia through her. Loneliness pushed her to climb on his body and hold on. She turned her attention to the box of decorations, pulling a string of garland from a plastic bag.

"Jennifer should be able to help you." She closed the lid on the box and sat the box on the floor. As long as she remained occupied she could forget him.

Instead of wearing a suit and tie, today, his dark jeans and cashmere sweater made him look even more handsome. She thought she might be able to get over him, but as he swaggered down the aisle to find Jennifer, she realized just how difficult getting over him was going to be.

The sound of his voice filtered to her, even though she couldn't make out the words.

He came back to the counter with a stack of books in his arms.

"What are you doing, Bishop?" She placed a hand on her hip.

"I want to buy these books."

She keyed up the register, picked up the first book and glanced at the title. "Why are you buying '*Love Letters of Great Men and The 50 Greatest Love Letters of All Time*'?"

"Maybe I'll learn something." He shoved one hand in his pocket. "I could learn all the right words and put them together just so that you know how I really feel about you. I hope they'll tell me the right way to win you back."

She rang up his sale and placed the book in the bag. "Bishop, please don't tease me."

"If you think I'm teasing you, then I really do need help with my words. I'm trying to get you to say you'll have dinner with me tonight. You see, I'm willing to go as fast or as slow as you want."

"But are you ready to go all the way?"

He bent and whispered, "I thought we already did that."

"I'm serious, Bishop."

"So am I. I've never been more serious. Dinner tonight? I'll pick you up at eight?" He looked determined. She felt like she was tumbling down a steep hill with her eyes squeezed too tight to grab hold on to anything to stop the fall. What advice would Mim give? She wanted to follow her heart, even if it didn't seem like wise choice.

"Bishop, we've been down this road, we know where this path leads. And as much as I might want to spend time with you, it's not a good idea. What's different now?"

"I am. I didn't think it was possible to miss someone so much. But all I do is think about you. Just have dinner with me tonight, that's all I'm asking."

She nodded slowly. "Okay."

§§§

Bishop charged to her door. This was the best he'd felt since storming out of her house. Every blood vessel in his body sang. Dakota had found her way into that place in his heart he didn't even know existed.

Watching Adanna with DJ, putting her son's needs before her own, melted Bishop's cold core. Her life was full and meaningful. She had people who anchored her, not a bunch of empty nights with names and faces she couldn't remember in a week. The closest he came to that kind of emotion was with Dakota.

He rang the doorbell and rubbed his hands together to warm them. He could hear her heels on the hardwood floor as she made her way to the door. His heart rate increased, like a kid expecting a surprise.

She opened the door and smiled at him. Her dark eyes met his. Before she could protest, he pulled her into his arms and captured her mouth. All he'd wanted for weeks was to taste her, touch her, and hold her. Now that he had just what he wanted, he couldn't let her go. She wrapped her arms around his waist, her breasts pressed against his chest.

After several moments, she pulled away and allowed him to step into the living room.

"Thank you for accepting my dinner invitation," he said.

She bit her bottom lip and nodded. "I'm not sure why I did. I'm even less sure why you asked me, since we agreed to go our separate ways."

"I'm not sure we agreed to that. You took a stand and made me accept your decision."

He sat on the sofa and she took the seat beside him. She turned towards him "Bishop, you made a decision about how you want to live your life. I made a decision about how I want to live mine. I didn't force my views on you because I respected what you needed."

For several seconds, he was quiet. "Dakota, I just want to be with you. You are the only person I think about, the only one I want to be with. I want to make a commitment to you. Right here and right now."

She searched his face without responding.

"Did you hear me? Aren't you going to say something?"

"You promised me dinner and I'm starved. What do I have to do to get some food?'

He reached for her hand and pulled her up off the sofa. "Let's go."

She grabbed her coat. "I think I better say this now, just in case."

"What?"

"I'm not sleeping with you tonight. No sex."

"I had no intentions of sleeping tonight. And what I want to do with you goes a long way beyond sex."

Chapter Twenty-Five

Bishop chose a small sushi restaurant in the city. They were seated in a circular booth along the back wall, facing the door. Bishop's thigh pressed against hers as he slid in next to her. He poured on the charm and she gathered her resolve so she wouldn't swoon.

The server showed up at their table to take their drink orders. "You'll love the martinis here. They make them great." Bishop pointed to the list of specialty drinks.

"I'll try a sour apple one." Dakota read from the menu.

"Make mine straight up, extra dirty." After the server walked away, Bishop turned his full attention on her. "So, how is business now that the renovation is complete?"

"Picking up. Some of the traffic is just for the holidays, but I believe many of the new customers will return." She swallowed. "You did a good job. I'm not sure I ever formally thanked you."

"I enjoyed every minute. Now, is there anything else I can do for you?"

"Let me think about it."

The server placed the drinks on the table and read the dinner specials.

"Can you order for both of us?" Dakota asked. "I always struggle on the right thing to order."

He placed an order for the chef's choice. "I hope you like sushi and sashimi."

"I've never tried raw fish, but everything you ordered sounds good," she paused. "Tell me what's really going on."

"I brought you to dinner to talk about us." The intensity in his voice matched the eagerness in his eyes.

"I want us to take our relationship slow. I never wanted to talk about forever, I just want to know if that's even a possibility for us."

"If I learned nothing else since I've met you, I learned that I don't want to be without you. My life lacked meaning. I'm much happier with you than I ever thought I could be. Probably more than I deserve."

Emotion clogged her throat. Instead of trying to respond, she smiled, daring a single tear to form in the corners of her eyes. Just hearing him say those few words made her heart swell with the love she had for him. If only she could tell him.

Dinner arrived. Bishop picked up a glob of wasabi with the end of a chopstick and stirred the green paste. He placed the shrimp tempura in the muddy mixture then positioned the piece on her plate before dropping a thick slice of ginger on top. "Go ahead. Taste it and tell me what you think."

After several tries she managed to pick up the shrimp with her chopsticks and take a bite. The strong essences of horseradish stung her nose, making her wince. "Wow." She managed a nod after several seconds.

"It's good, right?"

"Yes.

"Since we're taking our relationship slow, I don't want to assume you'll be my date at the Harper Christmas party. So let me ask you formally. Will you be my date?"

"You want me to be the girl on your arm?"

"I want you to be the woman in my life."

Dakota was afraid to meet his eyes, in case they didn't reflect sincerity. "How could you have changed your mind in a matter of weeks?"

"I don't want to lose you."

"So, if I was content to be a girlfriend for twenty years, then everything would have been okay?"

The stunned look on his face let her know her words had struck him. But she couldn't go running back with the giddiness of a school girl and no resolution. "Answer my question, Bishop."

"What does it matter? I'm asking for more. I want more, now, now.

She continued to run her finger around the rim of the martini glass. "Funny, how we've switched sides."

"We haven't switched. You don't believe me. I can tell when a woman is giving me the brush-off."

She didn't know how to reply. Instead, she stared off into the distance. This was too much. At first he didn't even recognize her, now he couldn't live without her. That only happened in movies.

"The Harper Enterprise Christmas party is next week, will you be my guest?" he asked again.

"Your guest or your date? There is a difference."

He scratched his head. "There isn't. For me, the words are the same."

"Your mother could be your guest, or your sister could. As your date, I'm the woman you want to spend your evening with. The one and only."

"Then please be my date."

She finished her dinner and pushed the plate away. The server removed the dishes and placed dessert menus in front of them.

"I can't eat another thing." She rubbed her tummy. "I'm full."

"You're not ready to end our date, are you?" Bishop winked.

She leaned across the table closer to him. "The evening consisted of dinner and nothing more. We aren't doing anything else."

"That's exactly what I had in mind. Take it slow."

She shook her head. "Bishop—"

"Okay, okay. We'll do things your way. I think I need to prove something to you and I will." He signaled for the check.

He escorted her out of the restaurant. All night he'd been attentive, as if whatever she said was exactly what he wanted to hear. She placed her hand over his. The warmth of his touch spread through her. The ride to her house was quiet.

He pulled up in front of the house and turned off the car. "I can kiss you, can't I?"

"Or I can kiss you." Dakota learned across the console and pressed her lips to his. He opened his mouth to accept her tongue. She tasted a hint of salt lingering on his tongue. He put his index finger under her chin to pull her closer.

She wanted to deny what was happening, but she would be lying to herself. She pulled away. "I better go inside before I get into trouble." She opened the car door before he could reply.

"Thanks for dinner." He held her hand and walked her to the door.

From the warmth of her living room she watched Bishop pull away from the curb before calling her sister. "Asa, I just had a date with Bishop."

"I thought you guys broke-up?"

"He showed up at the bookstore and told me he changed his mind. I don't know if I can believe him?"

"Suppose he's serious?"

She snickered. "Suppose he just doesn't like being turned away. He's trying to save face. Suppose we're just dating again?"

"Dakota, stop being so cynical. He might be sincere."

"He invited me to the Christmas party. As his date."

"You were already invited, so now you have a date. Isn't that great?" Asa sounded enthusiastic. "See you on Saturday. And Dakota please wear something festive. It's a party."

"Got it, Asa. Don't you have a dress I can wear that will make Bishop thankful to have me as his date?"

"I have just the thing. I'll send the dress over tomorrow."

Chapter Twenty-Six

Bishop glanced at Dakota's long, slender leg protruding from the high slit of her silky gown. The bright red color against her buttery complexion looked amazing. Her hair was pulled high on her head and diamond studs glistened from her ears. "You look gorgeous tonight. You should be on the Christmas cards."

She tried to cover her upper thigh. "You look quite magical yourself. But you always do."

At the Hotel DuPont, he pulled into the valet slot and waited while the attendant opened the car doors. This was his third Harper Christmas party, but it felt like the first. Tonight he wanted to make sure she had a good time. "Thank you for being my date tonight."

She slipped her arms though his. "How could I say no?"

From the lobby, they could hear the band playing. The holiday decorations amped up the celebratory feel for the night.

An attendant stepped up to them. "The coat check is to your right. Also, there is a picture booth to the right of the ballroom. Won't you please step that way to get your picture taken?"

"That's a nice surprise." Dakota clasped her hands together. "But who gets to keep the picture?"

"We'll share. You can have the photo for a month, then I have a turn for a mouth." He kissed her hand.

On the stairs leading to the Gold Ballroom, Bishop stood beside her. He wrapped his hand around her waist. Was there any doubt in her head that he wanted to be with her? Saying he loved her was difficult. Contee men didn't use those words. He chewed the inside of his cheek. If she needed to hear those words to know he wasn't just trying to charm her, then he would.

After the picture was taken, they were escorted to their reserved table. Several heads turned in their direction. Bishop pushed his head up and tightened his hand on her waist. Simeon and Asa were already seated.

"I knew that was the dress for you." Asa stood and hugged her sister.

"You look almost as good as my wife," Simeon said.

"Okay, you two. That's enough. This isn't the first time I've worn a dress."

"She looks stunning, doesn't she?" Bishop held her chair.

While they waited for dinner, Bishop caressed her knee under the table. He couldn't keep his hands off her. Life only seemed good when he was next to her. He had to find a way to make their relationship permanent.

His heart double-clutched as he stared at her. With his elbows on the table, he listened to Asa and Dakota talk about Mia. Dakota's face lit up when she learned her niece had taken her first step. The pure delight in her eyes was a look he wanted to see every day for the rest of his life.

He dropped his gaze down to her ring finger.

"Oh my," Asa uttered as she stared at the door.

Simeon turned around. "What is it?"

"It's Brian." Asa exhaled the words like she didn't like the taste of them.

Bishop felt Dakota's body stiffen as she turned to the door too.

It didn't take him more than a second to identify the long lost brother. He looked like an older version of Simeon, with a few more wrinkles and a lot less muscle. His graying hairline made him look older than he probably was, but several women turned to eye him.

Simeon rushed across the room and clutched his brother in a hug. "I can't believe this. What are you doing here?" Simeon sounded astonished.

"Surprise." Brian's extended his arms wide before his eyes landed on Dakota. He hugged Asa while staring at Dakota. "How are you, Dakota?"

Her eye twitched as she scratched the linen tablecloth. She looked at Bishop before responding. "Fine."

A stony silence fell over the table. Dakota dropped her eyes without acknowledging Bishop's hand on hers.

"Let me get another chair." Simeon pulled one from the adjacent table and put it between him and Bishop.

Dakota picked up her purse. "I'll be right back." The straight line of her lips coupled with her empty eyes told him more than he wanted to know.

Bishop pushed away from the table. A weight the size of a mountain sat on his chest. This wasn't the evening he'd planned and Brian's presence had all the makings to tear his dream away from his grasp.

§§§

Dakota rushed past the women touching up their make-up along the mirrored wall in the ladies room and closed the stall door behind her. She pressed against the metal door without turning the lock

How the hell did Brian dare stroll into the party like a returning hero? Her brain didn't register his face right away. It took several seconds before she realized the man crossing the large room wasn't an illusion, but her old lover. Her head whirled with questions. She choked out a hello, but nothing more. Yelling at him in front of the Harper employees wouldn't get her an invitation to another party. Her heart rate finally slowed. She stood straighter and shook the tension from her fingers.

Going back to the table or trying to enjoy the party was impossible. Sitting that close to Brian without reaching across the table and grabbing his neck wasn't going to happen. He owed her some answers, but she wasn't so sure she was prepared to get them tonight.

She opened the door to the small stall. The line of women had been replaced with a bunch of new recruits, but she found an empty space near the corner. After replacing her lip gloss, she pushed her shoulders back and marched out of the small restroom.

The activity in the ballroom hummed along as if nothing at all had happened. Didn't these people know a ghost was sitting in their mist?

"Dakota?"

She spun around to see Bishop. The dark glint in his eyes didn't make her want to run into his arms for consoling.

"What are you doing here?"

"I followed you, of course. Why did you run off like that? You looked like you were going to be sick." He reached out and touched her bare arm.

"I can't believe he could show up out of the blue like that. I just can't—"

"Why do you care where he goes?" His grip tightened on her arm.

She pushed a small tendril of hair away from her ear. Maybe she didn't hear Bishop correctly. "What? You think…"

"I think you shouldn't care about what he does or who he does it with. You said you were over him." His eyes accused her of something that violated her sense of fairness. She had every right to be upset. Not because she cared about him, but there were so many things she wanted answers to. How could Bishop not understand that? She'd have to be made of stone to pretend otherwise.

"Are you asking me to explain myself?" She leaned closer to him. "Because if you don't understand, then you don't know me as well as you think you do."

"What does that mean? This has nothing to do with me. What's happening here is about you and Brian. You have unfinished business with him."

She fought back the emotions building like a pressurized fire hose in her chest. She shouldn't direct her anger at Bishop, but she couldn't control the surge of emotion pulsing through her. The need to lash out pounded against her ribs and he was the nearest person.

"Don't you dare tell me what I should or should not feel! Nobody can do that. If you don't like my mood, then take me home." She paused for a moment. "No. In fact, take me home right now. I don't want to be around you, and I definitely don't want to be near Brian." She shoved her clutch under her arm and stormed toward the coat check.

Anger seeped from her pores like a fine mist. Her stilettos smacked against the tiled lobby accentuating her irritation. As soon as she had her coat, she didn't wait for the attendant to open the door, instead she snatched the handle.

Bishop came up behind her and handed the valet the ticket for the car. He crossed his thick arms over his chest. "Dakota, are you sure you want to go home? Your sister will be disappointed. If you have something to say to Brian, maybe now is the time to get everything off your chest."

She faced him. Everything he said was true, but she couldn't listen to his reasoning. Her head had disconnected from reality and was in a fog of emotion. She gulped in a deep breath of cold air. For once, she wasn't freezing. Her arms were hot.

"I just want to go home. Please, just take me home now."

Bishop's Lexus was brought up to the curb, the valet held the door open for her. She slid into the cold leather seat and buckled her seatbelt.

They drove across town in total silence. Even though they sat inches apart, the distance between them could have been the Grand Canyon.

When he pulled to a stop in front of the house, she didn't wait for him to open her car door.

"Good night, Dakota." He remained at the foot of the stairs.

At her front door, she turned to face him. Her anger subsided just enough to eliminate the red haze surrounding her. Tonight she could have used the comfort of his arms, but in all the drama of the evening, he'd been caught on the wrong side of the wall— siding against her. In just a few minutes, Brian had shaken her life up again.

"Bishop." She nodded her head, before opening the door and stepping inside. She watched Bishop hop in his car. She half wished he would pound on her door and say he understood her feelings, that no matter what, he'd always be there for her. Instead, he pulled away without a backwards glance.

Her phone started ringing the moment she stepped into the house. She checked the caller ID before picking up. "Asa?"

"Why did you run off? You didn't even say goodnight." Asa's voice registered alarm.

"Did you know he was coming?" Dakota demanded, her tone was short.

"If I did, I would have told you. I was as shocked as you."

Dakota sat on her bed. "Did Simeon know?"

"I'm sure he didn't. Brian thought his appearance would be a nice surprise. I think the surprise was you running out on him."

"Serves him right." She kicked off her shoes and stretched out on the bed. "If I said all the things I wanted to say to him, the image wouldn't have been a pretty picture. Harper employees deserve better than that. How long is he going to be here?"

"I have no idea. He didn't stay long after he realized you weren't coming back."

"What could he possibly want to say to me?" She rubbed her temples, hoping to push back the mounting pressure.

"I'm sure he'll let you know."

"Bishop thinks I left because I'm still interested in Brian. I think we're done."

"Done how? What do you mean?"

"He's left in a huff and good riddance to him."

"You don't mean that. I can tell you really like him."

"Give me a few months. I'll learn to mean every word. I'll be Mia's spinster aunt. The one who comes to live with her when I'm old and senile."

"Oh, boy. This sounds like a situation for a lot of chocolate. I'll be there tomorrow morning by noon. I'll bring the Godiva and the chocolate covered nuts," Asa said.

"I'll get up early and bake the brownies." Dakota sighed before she rested the receiver back in the cradle.

The phone rang again before she could slip the last shoulder strap down her arm. Without checking she picked up again. "What is it, Asa?"

He cleared his throat. Making the same sound from the beginning of the tape'd he sent to her. "Dakota, it's me, Brian."

She froze.

"Are you there?"

"I am." She sat on the edge of the bed, halfway out of the beautiful dress. The silky material covered one breast, the other was exposed.

"I was hoping to talk with you tonight. To explain—"

"Brian, I think you told me everything on your tape. I can't imagine you have anything else to say that I want to hear."

"I didn't want to break up with you. But I couldn't ask you to wait any longer. I could tell you were pulling away. I could hear the signs in your voice."

She crossed her arms over her chest, holding back the venom gathering in her chest. "Oh, you did that for me?"

"Can I come by? I'd like to talk with you in person."

"No, Brian. Everything you said was probably right. I was angry for a long time, but I buried my feelings. We don't need to rehash what could have been. You were probably much more honest on the tape than you could have ever been in person."

A long silence stretched between them. She could hear him breathing.

"Do you think we can be friends?" he asked. The tone of his voice changed. The tension gone.

"I do. We probably will make much better friends than we ever did lovers. Remember the first time we tried to make love and you—"

"I do and don't remind me. I was so embarrassed. I'd never had that problem before." His false chuckle hinted that the conversation was difficult for him too. "You might be right."

"Are you home for good?" she asked.

"No. I'm only here long enough to check on the mission, catch up with some of the men staying there, and then I'm leaving again."

"I should have known." He came home for the men at the mission, but not her. He should try the priesthood.

"Dakota, one thing I've found out about myself on this journey is that I'm never going to settle down. I'm terrified of being stationary. I believe if I stop or slow down, I'll turn into the kind of man no one likes. But I need your friendship. I always will." There was sincerity in his voice.

She hesitated a moment. "We've been friends since high school. We'll be friends forever. That's a promise."

"Have lunch with me tomorrow. Please."

This time she was quiet for a moment. How could all that anger disappear so quickly? She had wanted to scratch his eyes out and pound her fist in his chest. Where had all that rage gone?

"Let me think about it. I've got a date with a chocolate bar tomorrow." With that said, she hung up and pulled as the dress straps down her arm.

Dakota prepared for bed, the last vestiges of fury vanished. Her life was a revolving door. Brian walked out, Bishop stepped in. Bishop ran out, Brian strolled back in. And at the end of the night, she crawled into bed alone. She pulled the sheet and blanket over her head. All the stuff she thought she wanted to spew at Brian seemed unimportant now.

As much as she wanted to blame Brian for breaking up her and Bishop, she couldn't. The two of them were probably no better a match than she and Brian. What they had was fun for a while, but couldn't last a lifetime. Bishop wasn't that kind of man.

She turned off the light.

The phone rang again as darkness claimed the room. Cozy under the thick blanket, Dakota refused to lift the covers and allow the cool air to touch her skin.

The only people bold enough to call this late were her sisters or Bishop. Emotionally drained, she couldn't talk to another soul. Whatever physical fortitude she had left was reserved for sleep.

Chapter Twenty-Seven

Bishop gnawed the inside of his jaw as he sped away from Dakota's house. He understood why being single had to be ten times more hassle-free than trying to be with just one woman. In the past three months, Dakota had provided one hell of a rollercoaster ride.

But her reaction at seeing Brian pierced him like a poker through the heart. Just when he was ready to take the plunge and commit, she had emitted the smallest signal warning him away. The anger in her voice said she needed to calm down before they could talk. From the time it took to drive from the hotel to her home should have been enough, but at her door, she still wasn't prepared to discuss anything. Instead, she looked like a wounded animal ready to charge her prey. He wanted to fold her tiny frame in his arms and fight off whatever tore at the sparkle that usually burned in her eyes.

He made a wide U-turn at the intersection and headed back. Whatever was going on needed to be resolved tonight. He wouldn't let Brian tear her away so easily. At her door, he glanced up at the windows just in time to see the light in the bedroom go out.

The whole house was dark now. He leaned against the car and rubbed his chin. He fought back the urge to ring the doorbell, and got back in the car. Maybe a day or two wouldn't be too late.

§§§

Dakota hiked up her fuchsia flannel pajamas and jogged down the stairs. She pushed the thermostat up two degrees. If she planned to spend the day cozied in the house, the temperature needed to be warmer. Spending yesterday with Asa, eating chocolate, had been relaxing, but now she wanted some time alone. In the kitchen, she brewed a strong cup of coffee and pulled a pint of Greek yogurt out of the fridge. She hauled everything upstairs on a serving tray and dropped onto the bed.

The phone rang. She pulled it closer to check the caller ID. Bishop's name appeared on the screen. She propped up the pillows, ignoring him. How could she have fallen for someone like Bishop? He was only supposed to be the fun guy to help her forget about Brian. She wasn't supposed to fall in love. He kept his feelings tucked away somewhere safe and undetectable. Mim always said actions spoke louder than words. Judging from his actions, he cared about her. But her head needed to hear the words. Even if he only said them while whispering in

310

her ear in the dark of night when his passion had overwhelmed him.

She pulled the blanket over her bare feet and reached for her electronic reader. The letters of Voltaire held her attention until the phone rang again. Screening her calls wasn't mean, it was a necessity. Nothing would drag her out of the house today. Today was her day and she wanted to be alone, sorting her thoughts without persuasion.

Simeon's number flashed on the ID. "Good morning," she hesitated when she picked up.

"It's me, Brian. I'm staying here with Asa and Simeon. I was hoping I could talk with you."

"I'm listening."

"No, I want to talk to you in person. I think we've done enough talking on the phone."

"I'm not leaving the house today. It's a me day. I'm not even taking off my pajamas. Sorry."

"When do you think we can get together?" There was urgency to his request. Something she hadn't heard from him in the last year.

"Dakota, are you still there?" he asked when she didn't respond.

"Yes. Maybe tomorrow. Can we meet at the little café near Bookends? I'll be there at ten."

"Thanks, Dakota. I know this may be difficult for you."

"See you tomorrow, Brian." She placed the receiver on the nightstand and took a deep breath. Everybody wanted something from her. What she wanted was to tune out the world and hibernate. She needed was a little time to sort through the emotions without all the buzzing in her ear.

With her coffee cup in hand, she wiggled deeper in the bed and took a sip.

Chapter Twenty-Eight

Bishop woke with a start. He ran his hand over his chest, trying to move the heavy pressure bearing down on him. The room was still dark, but he was wide-awake. The alarm clock beside the bed registered six-thirty. Too early to call Dakota.

He climbed out of bed and parted the curtains. Off on the horizon, a sliver of light painted the sky a mixture of rose and blue. He continued to stare as night surrendered to day, mapping a plan to convince Dakota that they were meant to be together. As the sky brightened, he reinforced his belief that Dakota was his future. He couldn't let her slip away or return to Brian.

In his home office, he checked the clock every few minutes, waiting to call Dakota. The lump in his chest wouldn't go away until he heard her voice and smoothed everything out.

He picked up the phone, gripping the receiver in his palm. After releasing a heavy breath, he dialed her number. In each of his ears, his brothers shouted at him to put the phone down and run while he still could. But leaving Dakota wouldn't make him happy.

After several rings he hung up before the recorder came on. What he wanted to say, he'd tell her, not a recorder.

He dialed her number again. No answer. "Fine, Dakota. If you want to play this your way, then we will," he muttered as he grabbed his keys and headed to the door.

With a quick glance over his shoulder, he backed the car out of the space and pulled into traffic. This wasn't his first breakup, but never had one churned his stomach like this. He pressed the accelerator as he changed lanes and merged onto 95 South.

Monday morning traffic wasn't as heavy as he expected. He slowed a little as he made his way through Chester, but near the Delaware line the flow improved. He moved to the far left lane and tried to manage the speed limit.

He took the Route 273 exit and made his way to Mulberry. Catching her at the bookstore was best. She could refuse to open the door to her house, but Bookends would be open.

Across the street from the store he parked the car and surveyed the entrance for a few moments.

Once inside the store, he removed his coat, hoping to spot Dakota. Jennifer made her way to the front of the store, rubbing her right shoulder as she maneuvered through the new reading area.

"Good morning, Jennifer. Is Dakota in the back?" He started toward the rear of the store without waiting for a reply.

"She's not here. She called this morning and said she'd be in after lunch."

"That's a little strange. I've been dialing her number at home and she hasn't answered."

Jennifer lifted her right eyebrow and then turned her back to organize a stack of books behind the counter.

Bishop waited for her to turn back to him. The longer he waited the more interest she showed in making the stack neat. After several moments, he nodded and stepped outside.

From Jennifer's reaction she knew more about his relationship with Dakota than he'd thought. He rubbed his hands together to warm them. His breath froze with the crisp morning air.

Dakota's favorite café was only a block away. That shop had to be more welcoming than the frosty reception in Bookends. Running around town looking for a woman was out of his zone. If Adanna saw him right now, she would have a good laugh, and his brothers would revoke his birth certificate or scratch the Contee name from it.

He pulled open the door to the café. The strong smell of espresso filled the room. After ordering a double latte he moved to the end of the counter to wait for the disinterested barista to call his name.

Leaning against the counter, he spotted Dakota seated in the back at a small table. Her hair was pulled back in a sleek ponytail that revealed the earnest look in her eyes. Seated across from her was Brian. Bishop couldn't hear their conversation, but Dakota seemed intent on his every word.

Bishop shifted his position to get a better angle on her face. Her expression didn't change. Her hands were in her lap and a tall paper cup sat on the table in front of her. His stomach flopped. Almost without thinking, he made his way to Dakota's table. Without thinking what he would say when he got there, he cleared his throat.

Surprise twinkled in Dakota's eyes when she looked up at him. "Bishop, what are you doing here?" She pushed away from the table.

Bishop placed his hand on her shoulder to keep her in her seat. "Good morning, sweetheart." He leaned down and kissed her mouth. Consuming her lips in one deft movement. The sweet taste of her lips raced through him like a strike of lightning. She didn't resist as he placed his hand on her neck and pulled her closer.

Instead of taking her in the middle of the café, he released her mouth. "I called you a few times this morning. I need to talk with you. While I was waiting, I decided to get some coffee." He nodded to the front of the shop, where his name was being called. "Good morning, Brian. Nice to see you again." He stuck out his hand.

"Morning, Bishop. I just wanted to talk with Dakota for a few minutes. I hope you don't mind." Brian stood up.

Dakota looked at him and smiled. "Dakota is a grown woman. She doesn't answer to me." He rubbed his hand along her arm. "How about I wait for you back at Bookends?"

"Please, I should be there in a few minutes." She gave his hand a squeeze.

He kissed her again before walking away.

§§§

Dakota watched Bishop pick up his order and stroll out the door. Her chest inflated, as if she were being pumped full of air. His touch on her shoulder had warmed her in a way like nothing ever had.

"He seems like he cares about you." Brian picked up his cup and took a sip.

"He's very nice."

"How long have you two been together? Did you start—"

"No, Brian, I didn't start dating him until after you broke up with me, if that's what you're wondering. As a matter of fact, maybe your tape is what brought us together. I should thank you."

"The way he touched you and the way you looked at him. You two are in love, aren't you?" She picked up her coffee and held the cup between her palms. She glanced at Brian over the edge. "I don't think this is a conversation you and I should have. Besides, I can't speak for him. He's another man afraid of commitment." She wanted to admit she was in love, but Brian wasn't the one that needed that information.

"I guess I got my answer."

"Is it that obvious?"

"Yes. To me. You get that funny look in your eyes when you're pleased about something. You never gave that look to me, so I knew we never had a chance at anything permanent." He glanced out the window. "I'm sorry the way things happened between us. I hope you know my intention wasn't to hurt you. Never."

"Everything turned out for the best." She swirled the liquid in the cup to help cool it. "So how long are you staying around this time?"

"I'm leaving in two days. I hope to spend a little time with Simeon, Asa, and the baby before heading out."

They sat in silence a little longer. The only thing she could think about was getting back to the store and to Bishop, but he could wait for her for a change.

"Are you happy, Brian?"

He nodded. "I am. I know that might be hard to believe, but I really am. If I couldn't settle down for you, then I knew settling down wasn't possible for me. This is the life for me, as crazy as it may seem. But I want you to promise me something."

She placed her chin in the palm of her hand. "That all depends on what it is."

“Send me an invitation to the wedding.”

She leaned back. “Wedding? Bishop and I are a long way from discussing marriage.”

“Not as far as you may think.”

Chapter Twenty-Nine

Dakota kissed Brian on the cheek and skirted out of the café. Until she'd seen him at the celebration, she didn't recognize how the anger over their split had chomped at her spirit.

She wrapped her bright yellow scarf around her neck and hurried to Bookends. "He's here?" she asked when Jennifer looked up.

"Yeah, he's been hanging around all morning. Will you please put that man out of his misery?" Jennifer drew her mouth into a tightened frown. "He's in the back."

Dakota took a deep breath to compose herself before finding him.

"I want to apologize for the things I said the other night. I was probably a little more vocal than I needed to be."

He put up his hand. "Don't worry. I understand."

Without moving any closer, she looked him over, as if seeing him for the first time. Could she have a life with this good looking man who held her heart? "Don't you want to know what we were talking about over in the café?"

He stood up and reached for her hands. His long fingers closed over hers and he held them tight. "I only want to know if you need to tell me."

"I guess some people would call that closure. The things he wanted to say that weren't on the tape along with all my responses."

"Do you feel better?" He held her gaze.

She nodded. "I do. I didn't know I needed to have that conversation until we started talking." She paused. "You said you needed to talk to me. What about?"

Bishop moved to the tall wingback chair and crossed his legs.

"What are you reading?" She took the seat in front of him.

He closed the book and read the binder. " '*100 Best Love Poems of All Time.* '" A slow smile graced his face.

"Why in the world are you reading that? Are you trying to impress me?"

"Is it working?"

She didn't answer right away. Everything about him amazed her. He didn't need to change one thing, but his effort made her heart race. "Yes, it's working just fine." She removed her coat and scarf.

He pulled her into his lap and placed his mouth over hers before pressing his tongue into her mouth. She captured his tongue and deepened the kiss. After several minutes, she pulled away to catch her breath. Instead of releasing her, he continued to cradle her in his lap. "Did you come back to the store for me?" His eyes signal this was a big question for him.

"I don't know where we stand. I know you like being a playboy and having lots of women, but…" She stopped. Fear churned in her stomach. "I'm falling in love with you, Bishop. It wasn't supposed to happen. I tried to control myself. But…but…"

"I love you, Dakota." He stared at her. She drew back to see his full face.

"Do you know what you're saying? You don't have to say you love me, just because I said it to you. I'm a big girl."

"If you know nothing else about me, you should know I've always told you the truth. I'm a Contee and this is just as surprising to me as it is to you. But I've changed. Being with you has changed me. I only want to spend my time with you. You're the person who matters to me now."

She dropped her head on his chest and placed her hand over his heart. "Are you sure?"

"I just poured my heart out to you and that's all you have to say? I've never been more sure about anything."

"I love you too," she whispered.

"Are you just saying that because I just opened my heart to you?"

She whacked his chest with a playful swat. "You wish. You just might be in trouble now. I might stick to you like glue."

"Glue is good."

"Does this mean we're a couple now? Dating seriously?"

"No, this means you just agreed to marry me." He held her forearms while waiting for her to reply.

She opened her mouth, but snapped her lips shut again. Between the pounding of her heart and the whirling of her brain, she swallowed. "Marry?"

"You already agreed, so you can't take the words back."

"Did I say yes?" She could barely hear her own voice.

He pushed her sweater up and ran his index finger across her left breast. "You crossed your heart."

"And I would never go back on my word."

He stood and lifted her into his arms. "Let's go in your office. The doors lock."

"I have a better idea. Let's go back to my place. This might take a little time."

§§§

Bishop pushed up on one elbow to look down at the woman he'd just proposed to. How he could have fallen so quickly for her still surprised him. But every thought of her made his heart clutch into overdrive. Chasing women seemed silly now that his perfect match was nestled beside him, sleeping.

With the lightest touch he could manage, he ran his finger along her jaw, down her slender neck to the base of her throat. His finger settled into the dimple where her collarbones met.

325

She opened her eyes and snuggled closer to him. Her arm encircled his waist. "What are you doing awake?" The sleepy sound of her voice was sexy.

"Watching you." He enjoyed the warm softness of her skin.

"Is that all you want to do?"

"For now. Give me a minute and I'm sure I'll think of something." He massaged her breasts as his body readied to devour her.

"Should we think about setting a date?" he asked.

"You only asked me a few hours ago." She pushed up in the bed, allowing his hand to drop between her legs.

"Do you want a big traditional wedding with lots of attendants and even more flower girls?"

"I'm not pomp and circumstance. We could get married right here, if you could pull a minister from under the bed."

"Not while I'm making love to you. That wouldn't be appropriate." He slipped his finger into the moist folds between her legs. Her eyes were half closed as she threw back her head.

"We won't get much planning done if you continue to do that." She reached for his erection and ran her index finger around the rim of his swollen member.

After a full minute, he released her to grab her hand. Disappointment registered in her eyes. He pecked her on the check.

"You're right. Let's focus." He sat up in the bed. "I don't want to wait a year. I don't want to wait months. Do you think we can get married in a few weeks? I feel like I've dallied away enough time."

"All we need is a place, a cake, and some flowers." She tried to grab his member again, but he shifted away from her.

"Focus, Dakota. Family or no family?"

She hesitated for a moment. "I have to have my sisters there."

"Okay, your sisters and my sister. But not the whole family tree where we have aunts and uncles and long-lost cousins."

"That's fine with me. What about your parents?"

"My mother is a fan of yours, so I'll fly my parents in. Church or no church?"

"Church, definitely. I don't want my parents and grandparents to turn over in their graves."

"Babies or no babies?" He dropped his hand between her thighs again. She lifted her hips and parted her legs.

"What does that mean?" she asked as she pulled him closer.

"Do you want to start making our family now or wait until later? I might as well warn you, I want lots of children. Three, maybe four." He bent down to pull her nipple into his mouth.

She slid down in the bed. Before taking his hardened rod in her mouth she said, "We'd better get started then."

Epilogue

Dakota lowered her head to allow Melissa to adjust the short veil.

"Thank God I have well-organized sisters. There is no way Bishop and I could have pulled this off without you two." Dakota wrung her hands. Her straight floor-length dress was simple and elegant. Even the satin white shoes Asa had found were perfect.

"Dakota, you look absolutely beautiful." Asa swiped at the tear threatening to roll down her cheek.

"I can't believe you and Bishop are getting married. You've only known each other less than a year. Why the rush?" Melissa placed her hands on her hips, her nose pushed in the air.

"Stop it, Melissa," Asa warned. "I knew Eric for two years and we ended up divorced. Simeon and I were back together for only a few months and look how happy we are."

"Yeah, everyone is not like Darius. So put on your happy face and let's get me down the aisle."

Dakota had awakened with her stomach in knots. Never one to fret about minor stuff, this morning everything seemed to draw her attention. Instead of being there to comfort her, Bishop had spent the night in his condo. But this morning he sounded as calm as a summer day.

Asa handed her the bouquet of white roses. "See you at the altar."

Melissa reached over to reposition the pearls at Dakota's throat. "Just be happy, baby sister. Be happy," she whispered before following Asa out the door.

Dakota nodded as her sisters left the room.

One moment she was uncertain about her future and in walked Bishop with the strength and determination to make sense out of her life, pulling all the wayward threats into a nice tidy bow. She sniffed back tears of happiness.

"No crying today," she whispered as the wedding march began. She opened the door and made her way to the back of the church. The presence of her parents supported her as she squared her shoulders and started down the aisle. The glow on Bishop's face told her everything she needed to know. As she neared him, he reached for her hand and secured it in his.

JOIN THE JACKI KELLY NEWSLETTER
at

Jackikelly.com!

So you can stay tuned to new releases, appearance, and events and prizes. She's always giving something away.

Jacki Kelly has written dozens of short stories and several books. She lives in the North East with her husband and one loveable dog. She loves hearing from her readers so please contact her.

Connect with her online:

http://www.jackikelly.com

Twitter - @jackikellybooks

http://facebook.com/jackikellyauthor

If you enjoyed reading The Sweet Road To Love, please tell everyone you know. Please post a

review for other readers on your favorite reading
forum.

333

Trademarks Acknowledgment

The author acknowledges the trademark status and trademark owners of the following wordmarks mentioned in this work of fiction:

Volkswagen Beetle; Volkswagen Group

Brioni Roman Style Spa; Kering

Manolos; Manolo Blahnik

Gucci; The House of Gucci

Lexus; Toyota Motor Corporation

Barneys New York; Perry Capital

Saks; Saks Incorporated

HGTV; Scripps Networks Interactive

Styrofoam; The Dow Chemical Company

Whole Foods Market; Whole Foods Market IP, LP

iPad; Apple, Inc.

Sofitel; Accor Group

Duane Reade; Walgreen Company

Jaguar; Jaguar Land Rover Ltd

www.ingramcontent.com/pod-product-compliance
Lightning Source LLC
Chambersburg PA
CBHW032057180726
48284CB00002B/324